#ScaryWhiteFemales

A Novel

R. Scott Cornwell

For my mother.

On one issue, at least, men and women agree:
they both distrust women.

—H.L. Mencken

Table of Contents

CHAPTER 1

A more perfect union.

Framed by self-evident truths that all men are created equal; endowed by the Creator with the inalienable rights to life, liberty, and the pursuit of happiness. Government of, by, and for a people yearning to breathe free. A shining city on a hill; streets of gold by Pierre L'Enfant. The New Atlantis.

Washington, DC.

Beating heart of the corporatocracy. Government of, by, and for the connected. Eyes and ears of the surveillance state, whence your every move, your every utterance, your very *thoughts,* are tracked and stacked in the name of national security—loosely defined—and some amorphous war on terror. The happy marriage of medical technocrats and Big Pharma. Informing on your neighbor a civic duty. One's sacred honor (along with medical history) now the purview of the state; personal information by the ream feeding voracious databases courtesy of 300 million smartphones costing upwards of $1300 each. The swamp. Scene of high crimes and misdemeanors, favors bought and sold by elites flush with fiat cash. Engine of the self-driving war machine. Axis of the empire, where visitors from faraway lands pay state visits, and leave with marching orders. Where never is heard a discouraging word, the likes of which regarded now as sedition. And an alphabet's worth of entrenched bureaucrats sees to our well-being, thereby freeing everyday Americans from the rigors of self-determination.

And then there were the women.

Caught on a dozen or more security cameras, our improbable hero—self-possessed, droll, refractory in the eyes of his wife of forty-two years—emerged from the main entrance to that edifice of democracy, the Ronald Reagan Building. John Smith is 66, a huggable curmudgeon, realist-cum-idealist, nearing retirement and escape to Florida. Faded and rumpled, he wears the tired expression of one who suffereths fools not gladly; and the short-sleeved shirt and tie of the aging bureaucrat who never got the memo about a relaxed dress code.

He took a dim view of the gray sky. The "Accu" in AccuWeather was apt. It was drizzling for the eighth straight day, just like they had said it would. That particular day's event—in meteorological jargon they are known as events—lighter than that from the previous day but, rain or shine, the beaten raincoat was the call for late March and forty-seven degrees. He pulled the orange Orioles rain hat from the right pocket, and mashed it on the head closer to bald than he would ever admit.

His every step was recorded from multiple angles as he trudged up 14th Street.

All Men Are Guilty! It's OUR Time! The Patriarchy Shall Fall!

The banners so read. A group of women in rainbow "EMILY!" hats was distributing campaign literature. John politely declined. Unflappable as a general rule, he actually found these ladies quite frightening.

He was seized by the arm. Did he not comprehend, it was asked, that at the end of the day the result of one person's obdurate indifference was the further closing of the American mind—and the perpetuation of sexism and white privilege?

John had never gotten the white privilege thing. He couldn't remember anyone ever doing him any favors. Nightly he watched a medley of hysterical females and self-loathing males from CNN and MSNBC impute every vice, from original sin to algebra, from the founding to the present, on his kind.

He stood for the enslavement of women. "For shame!" Any shame felt by this particular white male, the consequence of his having been stuck in the same dreary job for more than forty years.

"You are the patriarchy!" an impassioned rainbow hat caterwauled as he moved on. Was he to fall? What might they do to him?

Reaching the intersection, he acknowledged a scruffy man in tattered clothing, a fixture on this corner. The sign that had been taped to the man's soggy sweatshirt had finally slipped off for good, held now in his left hand: Homeless Vet. Please Help. God Bless.

"How's business, Charlie?"

"You like the sweatshirt angle? I look more hard up without the raincoat." This professional panhandler, a master of his trade, and pinpoint market analysis, was brimming with the fruits of his labor. "No recession on this corner. I've had a helluva of a day."

"Charlie, you're a real entrepreneur."

"I just believe in people."

A well-dressed woman held a twenty. "Can you break this?" Charlie slipped the sign under his arm, whipped out a roll of cash, and counted out two fives. She held her hand out for more. He handed her another five. Put his hat over his heart. "Thank you, ma'am. God bless."

Benefactress out of earshot, Charlie replaced his hat and brandished the wad for John's benefit. "This month's car payment." He nodded in the direction of National Place, a large retail-office complex across the street. "You wouldn't believe what they charge for parking over there."

"What happens when they take us cashless, Charlie?" John inquired with the know-it-all smirk that drove his wife to distraction.

"By then I'll be off the grid."

Charlie was honest, in a Washington way. The two-bit hustler's venial sins dimmed in the glare of a ruling class that shook down the people with impunity, sneering all the while. Insiders, the elected and the unaccountable, lining their pockets as they waxed altruistic to a complicit media, and gullible public. Malfeasance couched in piety. The grander the larceny, the more respectable the crime. At least this ragtag outsider's marks gave of their own volition.

John nodded to his favorite street vendor, who slathered mustard on a Polish sausage and handed it to him.

"Put it on my account." They shared a laugh before John handed him a five, waving away the change.

"Whattaya doin' out in this weather, John?" Charlie wanted to know. "The Reagan's got a helluva food court."

John added onions from the vendor's cart, and took a bite. "Charlie, there's still that smell."

"Smell . . . what smell?"

John swallowed. "Washington."

He took another bite as Charlie watched traffic. "I'm ready to call it a day. Thinking about a new corner tomorrow. Eleventh and K. Maybe pick up a little convention business. An underserved sector."

He turned to see John walking away.

# # #

John took the Metro each day, not as any token of his virtue, but because the station was only a two-block walk, and he could read *The Washington Times* on the train. He hated the traffic. The truth was, he hated everything about the town. The tourists bugged him. Why didn't they go someplace worth their while? He detested the smug Washington countenance. All those people who thought they were so damned important. Smart, ambitious people did *not* go into government. Washington was for the lazy and self-interested. In Washington, stupidity got you *promoted*. Did these people not realize that America hates them? The whole place could go up in vapor, and the country wouldn't miss a beat. He hated most that he was one of them, except that he didn't feel important at all. He was embarrassed by his job at the Environmental Protection Agency. He had spent his afternoon harassing farmers in Iowa over the brand of fertilizer they used. Guys just trying to scratch out an honest living.

If this town didn't strip you of all delusion, you weren't paying attention. Impressionable youth, he and his future wife, Gert, did their sixties thing nearby at the University of Maryland. (The "sixties" being defined by those who make such designations as the years 1963 to 1973—the dawn of student activism.) U of Turtle had come late to the party, a veritable outback before impressive riots in the springs of '71 and '72 closed Route 1, made it big on the CBS Evening News with Walter Cronkite, and put the school on the counterculture map. *Terps.*

With John's Mensa grade IQ came an aversion to trying hard. So, not particularly ambitious, he had ended up in government, after two years as capable night cashier at the 7-Eleven. Ringing up the biker drunks who stumbled out of The Varsity Grill; or the entitled class, the Greeks, and the jocks who crawled up the hill from The Rendezvous Inn ("The Vous" to its loyal membership). The District of Columbia being only a few miles to the south, it was a mere hop, skip, and jump down Rhode Island Avenue to where the jobs were. The bureaucracy was burgeoning, and word around the Capital Area was that you could make good money for doing very little work, and retire early with a cool pension.

The hardest part of the early years was all the Redskin talk. A son of Baltimore, John repelled not so much by the team itself (actually he couldn't have cared less), but by their loathsome fans. Nowhere to be found while the team had languished, the diehards slithered out of the cracks the moment the team started winning. Didn't the whole world love the Skins? John wanted to gag. He couldn't so much as step from their rented flophouse in Hyattsville without hearing that stupid fight song playing somewhere. And why was George Allen constantly licking his fingers? It was not like he had to grip a ball or anything. A rabid Colt fan in his youth, John's exposure to Redskin fever at first strengthened his bond with the home team. But when he subsequently revamped his Sunday schedule, he decided the six hours formerly devoted to the Sunday doubleheader was time better spent in other pursuits; foremost, to catch up on his sleep. He preferred baseball, and Washington had lost its team again—Bob Short and his second installment of the Senators having blown for Texas. There *was* justice.

Gert's lifelong friend, Leslie, had turned John on to the opening at EPA, then still an inchoate federal agency, having been formed in 1970 after an executive order from President Nixon. The one decent act of his presidency in Leslie's opinion. She was thrilled with John's career choice—if it could have been called that—a place where he could make a difference. The Potomac River was in a wretched state, and John could be instrumental in saving it, and others. In John's considered view—and he had known her for more than forty years—Leslie was a left wing half-wit, whom were you to posit two plus two, would have a difficult time finding her way to four. And she only got dumber with age. She lived with her husband, Brock, in a trendy rundown house in the progressive ghetto of Takoma Park, Maryland, just over the DC line. After a second-rate career as a third-rate civil rights lawyer, Brock had been looking to make a name for himself at MSNBC.

The Vietnam War that he, Gert, and Leslie protested had been stupid and wasteful. John knew that. But forty-plus years on the inside had taught him that everything the federal government did was wasteful. It was no wonder we were $40 trillion in debt. Wasteful and unnecessary. Why couldn't the government just leave people alone? His cohort handed down edicts and interdicts with a callous disregard for the human consequences. If it concerned our precious Mother, the smart people at EPA knew best. John had happened upon the writings of H.L. Mencken, modern America's founding libertarian, and moved on from there, naively endeavoring to insinuate reason into the code; a conceit antithetical to the bureaucratic disposition. Amid the right-minded sheep in his department, he was the one in black. Playing out the string, he kept mainly to himself.

As he had awakened over the years, Gert had gone in the other direction, having surrendered her life to the triune god of pluralism, collectivism, and social justice. From inside the Beltway front lines, a *white knight*— **

** The narrator should endeavor to clarify that for Gert and her sisters this lamentable metaphor raises issues on a number of fronts. Starting with race. Where is it written that a man's skin color should render him ineligible for knighthood? An African Bavarian or Pacific Islander, for instance. Nowhere. Or in this day and age that women should be excluded? Hello. Furthermore, that this ill-advised word choice conjures images of the white knight coming to the aid of the damsel in distress. Excuse me, but we can take care of ourselves, thank you. The modern woman doesn't whimper, she roars. Which begs the question: what is there to ensure this character's nobility when he's off the clock? Nothing makes a dude hornier than riding to the rescue of a beautiful damsel. They are guys after all, and *no* man is to be trusted. #metoo.

—armed for battle with the purveyors of hate, confronting head-on every felony inequity foisted upon whatever less fortunate class at the hand of its white male oppressors. Leslie was Gert's lodestar, a conduit for misinformation, her finger on America's pulse, and the cultural sewer of toxic masculinity and racism. She was born woke. Not to be confused in any way, shape, or form with discerning. Leslie was feminist to the marrow, her life's mission to be a champion for equality, and to defy gender and ethnic stereotypes every day, in every way. She shared the care, and talked the talk. Or was it walked the walk? Walked the talk? John never could get them straight.

In endless confabulations fantasy was spun from fact. Leslie was all in on #metoo, and had stopped having sex with her husband. Gert, who had stopped having sex with her husband in the years preceding the reformation, had considered starting it up again so *she* could stop, but she wasn't exactly sure how to proceed with the plan, and it would probably entail going on a diet, which would most likely involve exercise, and her life was hard enough already. She didn't really think John cared either way. Leslie still a choice cut thanks to a vegan diet consisting mainly of water, sleep, and propaganda, John wondered how Brock was taking it. They had always been open about their rich and varied love life. Eavesdropping on multiple communications, John got the idea it was not going over well. He wouldn't mind doing Leslie, if he could shut her up for five minutes.

As the train lumbered on, John read from a story with the headline, "Benjamin Jamaal Singh Apologizes for Pantsuit Remark." Benjamin

Jamaal Singh was Emily Rogers Upton's rival for the Democratic presidential nomination.

# # #

His 2004 Bonneville was comfortable. It took a moment to find the proper setting for the drizzle that had turned to light rain. In John's estimation—speaking as a denizen of the Middle-Atlantic rainforest—pulse wipers were the previous century's greatest technological advance.

On the final leg of his commute, he listened as a nameless newsman delivered a report on the campaign.

"Still smarting from her latest primary defeat at the hands of Democratic front runner Benjamin Jamaal Singh, Emily Rogers Upton took her campaign to Pennsylvania today. She spoke at a rally in Allentown."

John cringed as he listened to the voice that grew more shrill by the day. "Americans want a president who's not afraid to take on Wall Street, or fight the Russians. With the foreign policy experience to do the job from day one. And never fear, Medicare for all is here. Thank you, and go Phillips . . . I mean *Phillies*." What sounded like a paltry crowd did its take on going wild.

The newsman continued. "She also dismissed a *New York Post* report of a romantic link between her husband, former Senate majority leader Phil Upton, and Nancy O'Leary, wife of Republican front runner, Jim O'Leary."

"There is no more truth to this rumor than there is to all the others."

A car passed John with an "EMILY!" rainbow bumper sticker.

# # #

There were nights the blatherskite was too much to bear, but that rainy evening found John in his recliner with his beer and cigar, set for a night surfing for *slants*—his politically astute father's appellative for corporate media news.

The room was old, the furniture worn; more fashionable decor materialism anathema to the virtuous Left. Only the leaders of the movement lived like royalty. His wife's home (he merely lived there) choked with the accoutrements of the pseudo-intellectual activist, to include her multi-cultural showcase, with folk art from three continents: African paintings and carvings; ersatz Incan, Aztec, and Mayan pottery; and Native American sculpture, baskets, and talismans. Her prized Frida Kahlo portrait. Stacks of progressive newsletters. Books, unread, but strewn about as if they had been. *Objets d'yard sales*. And the boxes—box upon box of heaven knows what. The *look* of Takoma Park, in prosaic Silver Spring.

Which suited John just fine. Unlike the Republicans he knew, he and Gert were debt-free, with gold and silver stashed in more of his idea of safe spaces than he could count. His recliner was sufficient to his needs, and forty inches of Sony flat-screen was plenty. He did get tired of falling over all the stuff.

Sarah Mills was reporting. "The Upton campaign issued an apology today for her remark that Benjamin Jamaal Singh has waffled on religion." Speaking over happy footage of candidate Upton, the reporter talked about her Democratic counterpart: "By now we're all familiar with the Ohio senator's background. The son of an African American father and Jewish mother, he was raised a Jew, converted to Islam in college, and ten years ago adopted the Hindu faith."

"A one-man melting pot." Though the house was otherwise empty, John would provide commentary.

Hips pushing the boundaries of her trademark pantsuit, 58-year-old Emily Upton spoke at a rally. For some reason she was wearing a Phillies cap, cocked to the side in an obvious attempt to look cute, but which in John's eyes made her look dopey. "Yes, it probably was in poor taste to question something as personal as my worthy opponent's religious faith, and for that I'm sorry."

Mills continued, speaking over the candidate's stock address. "The secretary of state, a former New Jersey senator, stressed that she was *not* a racist. She also said that it would be she who would stand the better chance in the general election against Jim O'Leary, because in addition to women, she is favored by working class, union, Catholic, Protestant, ethnic European, Jewish, Hispanic, Asian, and unemployed likely voters—as well as gays 25 to 54, transgenders, seniors, and those of no religious affiliation."

John weighed in. "And she's behind?"

Emily Rogers Upton waved to a make-believe crowd that wasn't there with her phony-baloney, high-wattage campaign smile.

The coverage cut to African American journalist Alan Winslow, reporting from the site of an enormous rally, attendees numbering into the thousands, shouting to make himself heard over the din. "Benjamin Jamaal Singh was on both the offensive and defensive today, attacking Emily Upton's politics of division in a speech before the Federation of Pennsylvania Teachers."

The candidate, slim and youthful, spoke before a CHANGE IS HOPE banner. "I am not a Muslim. I'm a Hindu."

"And he renewed his call for change."

"I'm not talking about chump change. I'm not talking about *pocket* change. A Universal Basic Income is real change. Am I right?" He stood back from the microphones, applauding his genius, before adding, "UBI, baby."

John loved politicians. Debt be damned, handing out entitlements like free candy.

She passed through the living room on her way to the kitchen, conveying grocery-laden canvas. Attractive in some distant past, the figure was fallen, her hair the gray favored by regenerate women who drive ancient Saabs and Volvos affixed with their beliefs.

"You're home early." Upbeat, their evenings usually starting *out* on a positive note.

"I had to get out of there."

"I wish you were more passionate about your work, John."

"Government doesn't work, Gert."

She spoke over the sounds of refrigerator and cabinets opening and closing. "Millie's home, and she sounds wonderful."

"Fresh outta rehab, ready to kick up her heels."

"She has a disease, John."

He watched 73-year-old Jim O'Leary responding to a question. What was it about the man that got under his skin? It went beyond his free college for all platform, or his lust for foreign blood.

His arm was around his wife. She was 37 and *hot* . . . several inches taller. Though his official bio listed O'Leary at five-nine, John didn't think he was an inch over five-six. He spoke through seemingly clenched teeth, words carefully measured. There was a noticeable tic on the left side of his face.

"With continued unrest in the Middle East, including the clear threat of a nuclear Iran, if American might should be called upon, I see nothing unreasonable in simultaneous intervention on multiple fronts," spoketh the patron saint of the military-industrial complex.

"O'Leary's got Little Man Syndrome. He wants to fight everybody."

"He's a war hero, John."

"So-called."

Prone to fits of patriotic ardor, and all but choking on stars and stripes, O'Leary reiterated classic neocon platitudes. "We have the strongest military in the world. How dare anyone, question, the courage and commitment of our brave men and women in uniform?"

"Pass the vomit bag."

Seethe was the word John was looking for. He had never seen any-one *seethe* like Jim O'Leary. The senator was asked about Russia, and the increased hostility between Moscow and the West.

"We have nothing to fear from a second-rate actor," the Republican candidate stated. "We stand ready to confront the Russian menace using any means necessary."

"What are you going to do, O'Leary," John nearly shouted, "nuke it out with Putin?"

"Settle yourself, John."

"The man's a maniac."

O'Leary's bellicose bilge was only the latest variation on an age-old theme. According to H.L. Mencken, wars were made, not by the brave, but by "demagogues infesting palaces." In 1939, as Franklin D. Roosevelt maneuvered America into yet another bloody, unnecessary war, Mencken wrote: "Whenever two gangs of thieves come into conflict anywhere in the world, it quickly appears that vital American interests are involved, and that unless one or the other gang is put down at once, not a sharecropper's wife in Arkansas will be safe from licentious generals." The more things change, the more they stay the same.

The final question for the Texas senator concerned the rumors about his wife, and former Senate majority leader Phil Upton. The right side of O'Leary's face began to twitch. "There certainly may be questions about Phil Upton's character, but as for my wife, Nancy, she is my lifemate . . . well, for the last four years anyway . . . and my soulmate, and I'll say noth-ing further." She winked for the reporters gathered, and planted one on his cheek.

Gert called from the kitchen in her irritating singsong fashion, "We have a new Latinx family on the block!"

"There goes the neighborhood."

"I know you just say that to get my goat, John. I can't wait to tell Leslie. You know how she calls this neighborhood the new Selma."

"She's a fine one. Her neighborhood's whiter than a picket fence. It's just full of people who think right."

He watched another report. Chicago Bulls superstar, Rasheed Williams, sat behind a bank of microphones. He read from a prepared statement in an athlete's halting monotone. "I want to offer my sincere and heartfelt apology for my remarks from the other night. In no way did I mean to offend any person, or persons, in the Little People community. We were coming off a tough loss, and I spoke in the heat of the moment when I referred to the Detroit Pistons and the referees as a, quote, bunch of midgets, end quote."

He turned to his legal cadre. Their heads nodded as one. "They beat us fair and square. I am sorry for any pain my tasteless remarks may have caused my teammates and coaches; the referees who do such an outstanding job; the people of Chicago and the greater Chicagoland area; the Detroit Pistons, their coaches and fans, the citizens of Detroit, and the people of Michigan; my friends and family; NBA fans around the world; and finally, the people of short stature I so callously offended. I let you all down. I eagerly anticipate my six weeks of sensitivity training which should be of lasting value in helping me relate to, and treat equally, all persons, regardless of age, race, gender, ethnicity, skin tone, national origin, religion, language, culture, family situation, sexual orientation, financial status, education level, occupation, or body type; particularly those smaller than I, facing a range of challenges unfamiliar to me, and those like me, blessed to play this great game. Thank you."

"That should pretty well cover it," said John, putting out his cigar. "And may Nike and my Chinese backers who have made me a billionaire please pardon my little indiscretion."

"Well, I think it's terrible what he said."

"A guy can't insult anybody—without offending *everybody*."

"You are so insensitive, John."

"Free speech for me, but not for thee."

Kitchen duties completed, she had entered the room, waving at nonexistent smoke, bound for the sectional. She settled amongst an ocean of pillows and heaved an outsized sigh.

"What's with you?"

"You don't even want to hear about the day I had."

She was right. He didn't. He turned off the TV and sat staring at the blank screen.

"What's the matter, John? Are you coming down with something? I don't know why at your age you're so hardheaded about getting a flu shot."

"I'm just tired."

"You've been rather remote lately. You know, there is such a thing as fear of intimacy disorder."

# # #

Gert sat at her vanity doing her face, with John propped up in bed, watching TV. "Did you put lotion on your hands?" she asked. "Lately they've been as dry as the Sahara."

He watched a commercial. A man sat right elbow to kitchen table, forehead buried in his palm, speaking to someone off camera. "Honey, these bank fees are killing us. And we're not making any money on our savings."

"You can thank the Federal Reserve for that," John remarked.

"And look at all these bills."

From the other room, SavvyWife had the answer. "Honey, we should go to Mid-Atlantic Tranquility Bank. At MATB the checking is absolutely free."

John reached for the lotion on the bedside table.

"Really?" replied CluelessHusband, father of three.

John squirted lotion onto his hands.

Eldest daughter, PreciousAndGifted, sat at the opposite end of the table, doing her homework. "Yeah, Dad. And at Mid-Atlantic Tranquility Bank you'll earn two percent interest on savings!"

"We're all gonna get rich," said John.

Middle daughter, CuteAndAmazing, chimed in from the living room. "And, Daddy, there are no ATM fees worldwide."

"Really!"

"How does this guy even find his way home?"

The sound of little footsteps preceded 3-year-old AwwwSheezSo-Adorable's flying leap from living room to kitchen—sticking the landing. "Ta-da-da-dahh. And at MATB you can pay all your bills online!"

"Wow. You are four smart girls!"

The dog barked. The close.

"That settles it. We're switching to Mid-Atlantic Tranquility Bank."

"Yay!" The girls jumped for joy—and all converged for a family hug. A sultry voice concluded, "Mid-Atlantic Tranquility Bank. Member FDIC."

John was rubbing. "Even the dog's smarter than this schlub."

"Maybe you should try that bank."

"If only *we* could be as smart as you girls."

"You've always been intimidated by strong women, John."

He went to turn off the lamp, but his hands were all gooey. He wiped them on his pajamas, and, having heard enough from strong women and smart girls for one night, turned off TV and lamp.

Gert finished and stood to face him, a robust figure in her nightgown. Whereas Leslie still had a waist, Gert had progressed to middle-aged lump stopover. "We need more African American friends."

"I don't lump my friends into categories."

"What have you *ever* done in the name of equity?"

"I pay the mortgage every month."

Oh, he thought he was so funny. "And you be nice to Millie tomorrow night. She's my baby sister."

"Your baby sister is a hopeless case."

She had a seat on the bed. "That's not true, John. Ted says The Meadows at Crystal Brook has been a godsend. He says Millie's a new person."

"There's another one, that Ted."

"Now what's wrong with Ted?" She changed her tune as she slid closer. "What's happened to us, John? We never laugh the way we used to. Are you having a midlife crisis? Is that what it is?"

What had happened to the sensitive man she married? The one who cared about fairness, and worked for justice. With his hair, had he lost his soul?

Everything had changed with the arrival of the boys. That was when he'd cut what was left of his hair, and shaved his beard. That was too bad. It made him look smarter. John Jr. and Mark made it three-on-one. Having sons brought out the latent machismo in her husband.

Born ballplayers, those two. For close to twenty years she tripped over bats and balls as they progressed from tee-ball sensations to all-county pitcher and shortstop, respectively. Somehow, the hypercompetitive world of baseball didn't mesh with liberal politics. She and the other moms hadn't lost their perspective, but at home they were drowning in testosterone. John lived for the boys—coaching, hitting grounders, throwing BP, and ferrying them to various camps. She and her surviving passion for activism took a back seat to the one in the bleachers.

But just as surely as that the games, and the schedules, had seemed to drag on into an indefinite future, her sons were off before she even knew what happened: John Jr. for Clemson, Mark for Virginia—Maryland's ACC rivals. John's loyalties divided when they came north to play the Terps. From their seats in ancient Shipley Field, mother lost in nostalgia for the halcyon days; father in mortal fear that John Jr. should hang a breaking ball, or slick-fielding Mark strike out looking. As long as Mark went three-for-four, or John pitched six strong innings, the old man didn't sweat it if their *teams* fell before The Turtle.

Each was now a respected member of his community, if not wellspring of angst for his mother. She couldn't blame them, of course, for their moral failings. John Jr. pitched, and then coached, for a number of years in the Reds' system, before selling out to Wall Street and settling down as a CFP in Cincinnati, preying on widows and orphans from a corner office downtown. He and his wife, Alice, had two little prospects of their own. She wasn't too sure about Alice, except that Alice *meant* well. As for John Jr.? He was just like his father.

After being told his bat had taken him as far as could be hoped, analytical Mark had weighed the pluses and minuses, and gone straight into coaching. Gert was proud of her younger son, now the head baseball coach at Forthampton College, but she had her doubts about Virginia. It was such a backward state. One of that son's first acts upon attaining majority being to join the NRA. The thought still gave her palpitations. Her little Mark had taken up with a dangerous crowd. He was a *hunter* now. She could just cry. He hadn't turned into a redneck or anything; after all, he came from good stock. At least on his mother's side. Still, there he was, ranging about the wilderness slaying defenseless animals—and carrying their carcasses home to his wife and children to *eat*. Ugh.

And it got worse. He and his wife, Nadine (who was a peach otherwise), had signed on with the Christian Right and were homeschooling their children! Poor Madison, Brodie (thank heaven for two girls), and George. What would become of them? It was the stuff of nightmares. It was said, however, that, unlike his father, little George with the quick bat could kill a fastball. Granddad (who was fine with the rest) was so proud.

Of late, there were more allegations regarding Nadine. She was an anti-vaxxer! What next? It was enough to drive an agnostic grandmother to prayer. At least neither son had ever asked for money.

Nest conspicuously empty, of bats and balls and boys, John had found solace in golf. She remembered how he came home all excited the day he finally broke 90. But golf was an elitist sport; white men, in oak-paneled clubhouses, behind stone walls. Tennis was so much more democratic. Tennis had the Williams sisters. Billie Jean and Martina. And Renée Richards! Pioneers. John was totally insensitive to the gender crisis. Golf had Tiger Woods, of course, but one man did not diversity make. And besides, he was a horndog like all the rest of them. With that fancy house and yacht, he was probably a Republican.

At least John wasn't a Republican. He called himself a libertarian. She wasn't sure that that might not be worse. They didn't seem to believe in much of anything. That horrible Fox News was wrong on all the important issues, but John didn't watch what he called the war channel much anymore. He got most of his information from the internet. That was where they had the real crazies.

She couldn't say she hadn't seen this coming. He had secretly voted for Reagan. Twice. She *knew* it. They had both hated Jimmy Carter, but Mondale hadn't been so bad.

Of ignoble origins, he really couldn't be blamed, growing up in Baltimore. Okay, he was from the *Timonium*, but still beneath her station. He hadn't had the advantages of growing up in Montgomery County the way she and Leslie had. Montgomery County schools were the best in the country. Everyone said so. John hated Montgomery County. She missed Bethesda, her ancestral home, but she knew John could never afford to move them there. Silver Spring would have to do.

At least John was clean. For all of his faults, he had always been clean; even back when smelling bad was part of the belief system. Leslie could, as John liked to put it, stand to lean a little harder into the shower. But then, Leslie had remained true to herself, and she knew John still lusted after her anyway.

Her husband began to snore—the state of his marriage no barrier to a restful eight hours.

CHAPTER 2

A man's home is his castle. Like most men forced to work for a living, to include those employed by government, John was a confirmed homebody. At home there was relative peace. The king was only second in command, but at least the situation could be managed. There was the easy chair in front of the TV, and the seductive solitude of his den. Even there ensconced, headphones were a haven. Under siege, beleaguered husband could always turn to old reliable, his *inner* mute button; and John tuned her out with the best of them.

Not that life on the home front came without pitfalls. Horticulture not John's bailiwick (and his being inclined to indolence), whatever yard work undertaken was, by convention, the minimum required to keep this homeowner one step ahead of the community association. "John's not handy around the house," Gert would tell friends; this little jab a thinly-veiled attempt to stimulate her layabout husband, but John was okay with it. *Project* was an abstraction, capricious in nature, given to leading the unschooled, and unwary, in dangerous directions. *Job*, his Monday through Friday employment. His man cave was the aforementioned den, his sanctum, where books overflowed shelves to be stacked on floors. There *was* a toolbox he last remembered seeing somewhere in the basement—to be opened only in the event of emergency. *If it ain't broke, don't fix it* was John's domestic policy, and he stuck to it. Carpentry? Plumbing? Not included in his limited skillset, such work was better left to professionals. With even the most basic of chores usually necessitating at least one trip to the hardware store, even these ate up a chunk of John's weekend he was loath to surrender. Besides, quality work could not be rushed. It had taken him five years to complete the paint job on the house's exterior trim ("By the time it's finished, you'll have to start over, John"), but he was pleased with the result. And she was always wanting to be moving furniture around; John, who valued stability, a believer in sticking with what works. On general principle it being incumbent upon the wife to keep her husband busy, it served John's interests whenever possible to be arriving home, just as she was leaving. Trips to the coffee shop or bookstore timed to coincide with her comings and goings ("I haven't seen you in at least a week, John)."

And beware the snares of consumerism. The Bible condemned materialism as idolatry, and that was good enough for John. The new Ultratec VersaPlexor S2Max had to be hauled home, room cleared for it, the assigned site swept and scrubbed, and the sorry old versaplexor retired. It had to be assembled, set up, connected, and instructions on the proper care and use of your new high-capacity Ultratec VersaPlexor S2Max reviewed. And, since it came from the new generation of *smart* versaplexors, it had to be programmed (the damnedest part), the warranty registered online, and so on. And finally, *versaplexors cost money*—and leave you holding a ton of useless cardboard. Give John the simple pleasures.

To venture out was to relinquish control. And anyway, for the most part, people were damned annoying. Were it not for the goading by the women in their lives, the outside world might never hear from working husbands. In John's case this applied, especially, to Gert's family. Her father had been a decent sort, but that mother. John would head for the hills; Pleasant Hills Golf Club that is, whenever the front was detected moving in his direction. Thank god for incontinence. The day they finally put her away had been one of dreams realized. Mother was still fussing and cussing at 91.

Gert's brother, Gerhard ("Hardy" to his loving sisters), was the tech geek. A hopeless neurotic, and decorated veteran of the war on speech, he was safely out of the picture, living somewhere in Silicon Valley with wife number four, the one who *finally* appreciated his gifts. Surrounded by three-quarters of the rest of the nation's oddballs.

Millie was Gert's project, her baby sister, as she would continually remind her husband. The fruit of their parents' last hurrah, Millie was the pretty one, a full seventeen years younger than Gert. She had issues, most stemming from having been spoiled rotten her entire life. More than pleasing to the eye, she had her way with men. Drank with impunity. She seemed to thrive on it, and, manipulatress that she was, could play the victim to a tee. And since she was a happy drunk, John saw no cause to rock the applecart. As he backed the car to the end of the driveway, he turned to his wife.

"Do we really have to do this?"

"I want to show our support for Millie."

"I've given up on Millie. I think the rest of the world should."

He turned down the street.

"Your seatbelt isn't buckled."

He steered with his knees while he buckled it.

"That's not safe, John."

After religion, nationalism being at the root of all evil, Gert was a committed *internationalist*. She went to great lengths to educate her hopelessly parochial husband. His mind had ceased growing by 30. If she could just get the *Baltimore* out of him. He was fixated on this H.L. Mencken, some dead, white, newspaperman. From Baltimore, where else. The most influential thinker of the twentieth century, John called him. Well, they were in a *new* century, and it was time to move forward. He would respond in his usual inane way that H.L. Mencken had spoken eternal truths. There existed Mencken societies all over the world, she was informed, but she didn't believe it.

He slowed to thirty as they passed a school, and fields of kids playing soccer. To Gert, sports were a waste of time—with one exception.

"Oh, look. *Futbol!*"

He wanted to throw her out the window. "Is it really necessary . . . ?"

"That's what it's called around the world, John. It's time you started thinking globally." She fanned herself with a road map from the door pocket, before reaching over and adjusting the temperature control. "Futbol is the international game. It's nice to see America finally catching up to the rest of the world."

"It's the mothers behind it," he complained. "To hit a little ball is hard. To kick a *big* ball, is not. It's good for little Johnny's self-esteem."

"You could just as easily have said little Jenny. Girls like to play too, John. On top of everything else, you're sexist."

He needed a vacation.

"And a xenophobe besides. Leslie calls you her favorite jingo."

"For every kid wasting his time playing soccer, that's one fewer kid playing a real sport. Like baseball."

"The white man's game."

"Whatever you say, dear."

"Maybe if you studied the sport a little, John. Learned some of its finer points . . ."

"Gert, five minutes of, *futbol*, and you've seen all there is to see. Every game ends one–nothing."

"That's one-nil."

"They should flip a coin, decide who gets the one, and spare us the three hours of back and forth."

"It wouldn't hurt you to learn about other cultures."

"I'm still trying to make sense of this one."

He turned onto East-West Highway, filled with late rush hour traffic. Looked over at Gert, nose in her phone. He hated the damn things—smart people did not need smart *phones*—but at least it kept her occupied, and off his back.

Yet, he couldn't resist. "You know, that thing gives off electromagnetic frequencies, proven in laboratory studies to alter living cells. Cells like, brain cells?"

"You'd have us go back to town criers."

"I can visit you in the sanitarium. They have a nice room where you can bang your head on the rubber furniture. They'll teach you happy games, and you get to play with pretty blocks and learn your colors."

He was forced to brake abruptly as another car cut him off. "People have no idea how to change lanes."

"And of course, you do."

Her eyes had not strayed from her device. He gave it another moment. "You realize, they know everything about you."

"Who is they?"

"Big Brother."

Her apostate husband, who stood for nothing, could fall for anything. Law-abiding citizens who respected the environment, and wanted to tear *down* the walls separating us, had nothing to fear from some imagined Big Brother. "What interest could your Big Brother possibly have in a text from Leslie?"

"Hah-hah," her husband laughed. "That very security apparatus exists for such as Leslie."

"You're starting to sound like all those other conspiracy kooks." She went back to the phone, reconsidered, and put it back in her purse. "I don't feel like dealing with her now anyway."

For several moments they rode in blessed silence. At one one-thousand-four—

"She took me for a ride the other day in their new Prius."

"Here we go . . ."

"It's great on gas, and much better for the environment. Certainly better than this old Pontiac." She held a protective handkerchief over her nose and mouth.

"This car runs like a top."

"They don't even *make* them anymore," his long-suffering wife's retort, muffled from behind the handkerchief. "It's like riding around in my grandfather's Packard."

How could she take another minute? Here was her husband, privy to forty years' worth of data, and he had not lost so much as an ounce of sleep over the poison spewing from that old jalopy.

"Besides, it's paid for."

"If you took your career more seriously, John, we could afford to buy a green car. You should have made department head a long time ago." She lowered the visor to check her face in the mirror. "And don't forget your cholesterol tonight. I know you love Ted's cooking, but that belt of fat around your middle can shorten your life span."

"I don't see you on any magazine covers."

"It's especially dangerous in males. You know you don't get enough exercise, John."

"I get all the exercise I need on the golf course."

"Your turn signal is on. You can't hear that?" She sighed in her exasperation. "You really should have your hearing checked."

# # #

Ted and Millie's house in Bethesda was larger, grander, and in a much better neighborhood than theirs, as Gert was wont to remind him. Ted was a ninety-eight-pound weakling who had made it as some sort of researcher at NIH. As John looked around the lavish dining room, he wondered what Ted made. Enough, apparently, to afford a house like that and still support his wife's hobby.

He sat proudly at the head of the table, John and Gert on his either side, under a magnificent crystal chandelier. He was high on life in light of that wife's most recent recovery. She came through the swinging door from the kitchen carrying a roast on a silver platter; John struck anew by her beauty, as he was every time he saw her. She paused for a moment, looking unsure of herself.

"Ooh. Felt a little dizzy there for a moment." She placed the platter before her husband, and headed back into the kitchen. As he began to carve, Ted directed his remarks to his faithful sister-in-law, his rock through the ups and downs of addiction.

"Do you sense the serenity?"

They were startled by the sound of shattering glass that came from the kitchen.

"Oh, let me see what she's up to," said Ted pleasantly, one patient man passing through that door. He loves her so much, thought Gert. Knowing her husband's skepticism, she made a point of looking everywhere but at him. She just wished he could be a little more *feeling*.

How had the girl who should have married the quarterback ended up with this wonk? said unfeeling husband was wondering. A brain-damaged football player would have been more on Millie's intellectual plane. Ted he could fathom. Millie was a piece. Measured against the great mismatches, theirs stood the test.

They heard laughter from the kitchen.

Ted returned, all smiles, carrying a pitcher of ice water, and filled their glasses. "A little accident. No harm done." He spoke apologetically, "Normally an occasion such as this would call for some wine, but under the circumstances..."

Gert reached out and tenderly patted his hand before he resumed his carving. "Do you see the difference?" He stopped to address them. "In the past, a little kitchen mishap would have sent her into a tailspin, but not the new Millie."

Gert was already won over. "She's almost... blissful."

"Dr. Saperstein is a miracle worker."

Millie emerged from the kitchen with a covered dish of potatoes—"Ooh, hot-hot-hot!"—virtually dropping it on the table. "*Loved* Dr. Saperstein." This with a dreamy smile, and a wink for John, as she returned to the kitchen.

Ted went back to his carving. "What sets The Meadows at Crystal Brook apart is their nonjudgmental approach."

"It's no sin to have a disease." John was dealt a look.

"Exactly. In the past, some of Millie's other... retreats... have left her with a tremendous burden of guilt."

Gert shook her head sadly. They were always so hard on dear Millie. "Remember that awful therapist at The Meadows at Fairhaven?"

"Mmm. That was The Meadows at *Blue Vista*," Ted corrected.

"Millie's entire life has been spent in denial of self."

"Along with various clinics," John volunteered, joining the conversation. Ironic, listening to those two assessing denial.

Ted was nodding. "Identity issues. Dr. Saperstein focused on those."

"What some see as her fundamental reserve is, in reality, a suppression of all that is Millie." How had they been so blind to Millie's suffering all those years? Tears streaked big sister's plump cheeks.

"And with suppression . . . comes regression," Ted added clinically.

"She yearns for self-expression!"

"She tends to internalize, rather than verbalize."

"Which, in turn, diminishes her coping skills."

"The doctor said that's typical in the daughters of disengaged fathers and controlling mothers."

"Mother did her best, but Dad did have a tendency to withdraw."

John, recalling how suicide had been intimated in the old man's ultimate withdrawal, was on the receiving end of a pointed glance.

"Your father was the enabler," said Ted soberly.

"Precisely."

"And a generation later . . ."

Psychobabble spiraling out of control, John stepped in before someone got hurt.

"I think she just likes to drink."

Gert recoiled in horror. The man was beneath contempt. How could she ever have married such a brute? She hoped she wasn't going to hyperventilate. That happened sometimes.

Ted was on a roll. "River Oaks was where we first saw encouraging signs. But Millie's time at the Brook has been life-changing. She's reached a whole new level with Dr. Saperstein and his Time Out therapy."

Millie swung in carrying a gravy boat. "Mmmm. Dr. Saperstein is a genius." As she placed the dish of gravy on the table, she momentarily lost her balance, spilling some. "Oh, dear." With a flip of her hair she breezed back to the kitchen, humming sweetly.

Ted was ebullient. "Do you see?"

"She's at perfect peace."

Millie returned with a sponge and wiped up the spilled gravy. John was taking it all in. As she went to leave, she knocked over his water glass. "Uh-oh," she said, the way a two-year-old might. She was giggling at some private joke as she returned to the kitchen. John soaked up the spill with his napkin.

Gert was all bubbly. "So tell me about this Time Out therapy."

Carving finished, Ted took his seat, basking in the spotlight. Happy, carefree days lay ahead. "The key to treating this disease is dealing with the inevitable setbacks."

"Is she on any medication?"

"None. That's the beauty of Time Out therapy. It goes straight to the root of the problem . . . to her deepest sense of self." Gert smiled sweetly, nodding in agreement. Speaking of timeouts, John wondered, where the hell was dinner?

"In a moment of weakness, when her equilibrium is upset, when all may be in danger of slipping away . . . she simply calls Time Out."

Gert was transfixed. "Yes," she whispered. The simplicity was profound; and it had been right there in front of them all along.

"You take a deep breath. Stand back and reflect. Process your feelings."

John looked curiously toward the kitchen. "Speaking of which, I'm feeling mighty hungry." He refilled his water glass.

"The restorative powers of the time-out are amazing. It *becomes* your escape mechanism."

"The man is a genius."

Ted marveled at secrets revealed. "She's experiencing a whole new sense of freedom."

His other guest conspicuously squirming, Ted finally looked in the direction of the kitchen. "Are you okay in there, hon?"

Silence.

"Mill . . . ?"

Nothing. "Excuse me for a moment." He got up, throwing down his napkin, and returned to the kitchen. John leaned across the table.

"She's hammered."

"What?"

"She is *hammered*."

"What do you mean . . . hammered?"

"What do you think?"

The directive came from the other side of the swinging door. "*Time . . . Out . . . Millie.*"

With his hands, John formed the T for those at the table.

"Take a *deep breath*."

"A little late for that."

Her haunting laughter resounded throughout the house. Ted stormed through the dining room with the evidence, and out the front door. Multiple times out had furnished Millie time ample to exhaust the entire contents. They heard the car start up—and peel out.

"She can put it away."

He looked across at big sister, stricken by this latest tragedy.

"Is this a setback?"

# # #

Gert listened to her beloved Tom Morrow as she prepared breakfast. "For National Public Radio I'm Tom Morrow saying until next time, and reminding you, my faithful listeners, we must move fo-ward."

John hurried in, a number of envelopes in his hand, and changed the station. John detested Tom Morrow. Tom Morrow was the radio voice of the educated idiot. And the effusion of self-love in that patronizing farewell exceeded even that which John's famously open mind could allow.

"WTOP News time, 6:55."

He placed the envelopes on the counter. "Can you mail these?"

"If you insist. I don't know why you can't pay our bills electronically, like everyone else in the civilized world." They were living in the Dark Ages.

He took a cup from the top shelf of the cupboard, along with a glass from the lower. He held the empty glass in his hand, performing studied inspection. "Are these new?"

"Why, yes, they are." She was pleased. "I can't believe you noticed."

"What was wrong with the old ones?"

"I was *tired* of them."

Perfectly good glasses. He poured himself some coffee, and dumped the filter and grounds in a handy receptacle.

"That's the recycling, John." He added milk and sugar, grinning as he stirred. "You do that on purpose." She closed the cupboard. "And do you ever close a cabinet?"

"Who was on the phone?"

"It was Ted." She slumped to her very core. "Millie confessed to having an affair with Dr. Saperstein."

"The miracle worker."

She set their plates on the table and collapsed on a cataract of tears. "Poor Millie."

"Poor *Millie*?"

He shook his head—purging the madness—and took his seat, lost for words, if not appetite. He salted his omelet and started shoveling.

"You could at least taste it first," she sniffed.

She sat, despondent. Of a sudden her eyes brightened. She had looked inward and found hope. "But you know what, John? Millie's a strong woman. She'll get through this."

From the radio came a report: "Presumptive Republican presidential nominee Jim O'Leary is defending himself against comments that he sees a terrorist under every bed."

As he listened, an acute loathing arose in John. "Simply because we haven't experienced a major terrorist attack on American soil in more than a decade is no reason to let our guard down," said the Paul Revere of Terror, Islamic and otherwise. "This is a war that will go on for generations, and I'm prepared and willing to lead the fight."

Gert dried residual tears. "Will you be able to hang it tonight?"

"Somebody should hang him," said her husband, alluding to his bête noire. He thought for a moment. "What was it H.L. Mencken said about politicians . . . how they create an endless series of hobgoblins, all of them imaginary?"

"You and your Mencken." She turned her attention back to important matters. "I'd like to have it up in time for our dinner with the Padillas."

John popped a sausage in his mouth. "Who the hell are the Padillas?"

"Our new neighbors up the street. Do you never listen to anything I say?"

"Remind me why we're having dinner with perfect strangers?"

"I want to welcome them to the neighborhood, John." A social imperative. "And demonstrate our commitment to diversity."

He implored the cracked ceiling. He was inured to his wife's well-meanings, but only so long as she didn't rope him into the exercise. "Is this hospitality, or a political statement?" Spoken from a mouth stuffed with egg.

"Your cynicism is growing tiresome, John."

"And the Texas senator bristled at reports that his wife, Nancy, and former Senate majority leader Phil Upton were seen yesterday leaving through the rear door of The Mayflower Hotel. Campaigning in Pennsylvania, Democratic candidate Emily Upton declined comment."

John laughed. "Aw, they're *lonely*." Nobody could charge him with being insensitive.

The newsman continued. "Locally here in the Washington area, March is Minority Mental Health Awareness Month. In a coordinated effort between leaders in The District, Maryland, and Virginia—"

"Who the hell comes up with this stuff?"

"Oh, hush . . . Do you think of nothing besides your stomach?"

He started to ask—

"By the way," she continued, "have we decided where we're going to spend our vacation?"

If he had any say in it, they'd just stay home. Whoever had invented the staycation had been on to something. "You mean, have *you* decided where we're going to spend our vacation?"

"I think we should make plans."

"Gert, I beg you. No more exhausting vacations."

CHAPTER 3

S he resented the implication. That misadventures from past vacations were the result of faulty planning on her part. She worked hard setting up their trips, knowing that if it were left to him every vacation would find them on Fenwick Island, or visiting the boys. She loved her sons (and of course her grandchildren!) as much as any woman, but suburban Ohio, and Roanoke, Virginia, were perfectly lovely places to raise families, not exotic destinations. How many Reds games had she been dragged to? Let the boys visit *them*. And after the Boston debacle she had had it for good with baseball vacations.

It should have been a perfectly lovely trip to Massachusetts the previous June. With John's passion for American history, and her love of New England, Boston and the surrounding area had seemed a perfect fit for a ten-day trip. She even managed to secure tickets to two Orioles-Red Sox games at Fenway Park. Purchased through a broker. What did he expect, that travel sites should post *warnings* that the dates she had chosen coincided with Pride Week?

And what a spectacle it was! The color; the pageantry; the love; and her husband barricaded inside their hotel room. On the phone with everyone from the airline to the hotel, demanding refunds. Why couldn't he embrace those different from himself?

"I'm afraid to even shake their hands."

Manifest ignorance. Her very own Archie Bunker could have chosen to make it an educational experience, but he was too thick-headed. Well, it hadn't stopped her. She learned firsthand more than she ever could have imagined about the persecution of her LGBT brothers and sisters, and their brave struggle for equality.

"What persecution?" he had asked. "They've taken over."

"Where's your empathy, John?" She was appalled on the inside, and humiliated on the outside, by her husband's homophobia. She couldn't take him anywhere. Despite her assurances that AIDS and hepatitis were not airborne viruses, he had literally run for that cab to the ballpark. Only that silly blood test on their return home had allayed his paranoia.

Nor could she be held accountable for the vicissitudes of the weather in a period of climate change. The previous February, after Maryland was hit by a series of brutal snow and ice storms, Southern California had seemed like a perfect getaway. Leslie and Brock had returned from nine sublime days in San Diego working in support of the homeless. A sun-bronzed Leslie spoke of glorious sunshine and temperatures in the seventies. What a beautiful place, and with so many progressives! Gert told John to dust off his clubs, they were heading west.

They made it as far as Denver; where a blizzard of biblical proportions had socked the Mile High City. The storm, of such intensity that all flights were immediately grounded and incoming flights diverted, began within minutes of their arrival, reducing visibility to zero, dumping thirty-nine inches of snow, and stranding them at the airport Hilton. Freakishly warm temperatures the next day had triggered massive flooding, followed by an Alaskan front and hard freeze. From their window at the Hilton, John watched crews with picks hacking through ice as much as eighteen inches thick. It was five days before the next flight, but he told Gert he was adapting to vacations spent in hotel rooms. It was the next best thing to staying home.

She was becoming desperate in her attempts to reclaim her dissident husband, but Leslie convinced her she was on the wrong track. *Incrementalism* was the only approach in tough cases like John's. It was working around the world. They had not lost him overnight; winning him back would take time. Gert was never to give up hope. Her husband being simple-minded and base in his tastes, his receptors were not keen to subtle manipulation. The cultivation of a citizen of the world called for the careful tilling of rich soil, abundant rain, and sunshine for the soul. In John's case, in the forms of good food, salubrious weather, and golf.

The first of these had been the trip of a lifetime down the Amazon. Like most climate deniers, John was also willfully ignorant regarding the denuding greedy developers were perpetrating on the rainforests. Gert and Leslie knew deforestation, should he witness it for himself, might enlist him to the cause.

A perfectly understandable miscalculation on her part may have been partly to blame for the trip down the river not going exactly as planned. March, being late summer in the other hemisphere, Gert made the reasonable assumption that summer would be the dry season; like it was everywhere else in the world. Well, it turned out that summer was actually the wet season. It rained all the time, but summer was the worst, and that particular summer had been the wettest in decades.

John being already in foul humor after the bumpy flight through the mountains in an aging biplane—

"That could have gotten us killed, Gert."

"Oh, John, you exaggerate."

—it was a blessing that morning in Iquitos had dawned sunny and delightfully cool for their first day down the river. The sights were breathtaking from the deck of the first-class riverboat. Even John seemed caught up in the experience.

Then it began to rain. And the river started to rise. After "one hell of a ride" they made it safely to their night's lodging in that charming Peruvian river village. Most fortunate in that their room was on the top floor of the little inn; by midnight the first two floors being underwater. They were two days without power, but there had been a bunch of bananas, compliments of management; a leftover box of crackers; and plenty of warm bottled water in the refrigerator to go with the well-stocked bar.

On the third day they were rescued. Inauspiciously, Gert's high school Spanish proved of little avail communicating with their Portuguese-speaking rescuers. What was finally made clear by the boat captain, fluent in broken English, was that she and her hopelessly hungover husband were to be airlifted, courtesy of the American Embassy in Lima, and carried to safety in the capital by helicopter. Gert was a hit on CNN with her passionate appeal on behalf of the rainforests, and John—fully recovered by then—was something of a celebrity in the agency upon his return.

Gert saw no reason why this latest trip should not be part of the process. She sat at the dining room table in a frayed duster. She had been waiting for her husband to notice the sorry state of her nightwear, but, as in all things, he was oblivious. It was after one in the afternoon, but she liked to finish her housework before she dressed. She was on her laptop, typing and clicking, working on a plate of gluten-free waffles.

And she had found it.

Talking to oneself one of those habits one acquires from one's spouse, she read aloud. "'North America's Progressive Vacation Destination.' Ooh, I like the sound of that." She took a drink of Smartwater. "Behold the breathtaking beauty of the Oregon coast at this one-of-a-kind retreat.

Nestled among towering pines, overlooking the rocky shoreline and blue Pacific. Experience Nature in all Her grandeur, in a pristine environment unspoiled by man's influences. Come to Progress, Oregon—*the perfect romantic getaway!*'"

She scrolled down. Smiled. "Seven days in Progress, Oregon. Six nights. Including airfare . . ."

# # #

He supported an oversized picture frame; in front of him the space on the wall empty but for two waiting hooks.

"But it's the first thing people will see when they walk in."

She was the lady of the house; and she was unbending. Exhaling heavily, John lifted the frame by the bottom corners—and hung a copy of the vice-presidential portrait of Al Gore. "From now on everyone comes in through the garage."

Gert gazed reverentially at the portrait. "A life serving humanity."

"Otherwise known as fattening up on the lecture circuit."

"Winner of the Nobel Prize. And don't you dare be looking at my middle when you make such a remark."

He straightened it, and stepped back for further examination. "'The demagogue is one who preaches doctrines he knows to be untrue, to men he knows to be idiots.'"

"John, your very soul has been poisoned by H.L. Mencken."

He had a final, tortured, glimpse of the portrait. "I've gotta get away."

She followed him into the living room. "On that very subject . . ."

He picked up his *Washington Times* and had a seat in his recliner, right ankle over left knee, displaying an argyle sock of regrettable green and purple. She hovered, dronelike. "Where in heaven's name did you find such hideous socks?"

He glanced at his sock, and resumed his reading.

She was about to burst. "I had a *find* today."

He turned a page. "Can't wait to hear this . . ."

"Progress, Oregon."

Her wary husband's eyes never strayed from his paper. "We're going on a tour of lumber mills? I thought you hated the timber industry."

"I'm *sharing* with you, John. Would you please keep an open mind?"

He gazed up at her. "I just hung . . . a portrait of Al Gore."

She had always been one who gave credit where it was due. "A sign of your growth, I will admit." With Leslie whispering in her ear—*incrementalism*—maybe that had been enough for one night.

But he wasn't finished. "They should string up all the politicians. And they can start with Al Gore."

That could not be allowed to pass. "He's only trying to save a planet."

"'The urge to save humanity is almost always a false front for the urge to rule.'"

"Well, H.L. Mencken didn't know the vice president."

John chuckled dryly. "Yes, he did."

Oh, he thought he was so clever with his armchair potshots. She stood her ground as he leafed through the paper. He finally looked up. "What?"

"Progress. Oregon."

He turned back to his paper. "That word sends chills down my spine."

"Oh for heaven's sake. We have to move *forward*, John."

He dropped the paper in his lap. "Why is it always the further forward we move, the worse things get?"

She handed him the printout. He read it and handed it back. "You see, we're not Americans anymore, we're North Americans."

"*Try* thinking globally, John."

She had him take another look. He saw nothing but red. "This progressive business scares the shit outta me."

"Oh good gracious . . ."

Snow-choked airports and helicopter rescues leapt to mind. This place was wrong, he *felt* it, like recurring Andean airsickness. "Why do I see us in the woods, foraging for roots and berries, and bathing in the nearest body of freshwater?"

"It's a four-star resort, John."

So that was it. "Well, in that case we can't afford it." If there was one thing you could count on, these left-wing loons were never shy about redistributing wealth from your pocket, to theirs. They overcame alright.

She happily tapped a spot on the printout. The price he saw, which included airfare, was clearly too good to be true.

"Shouldn't this tell you something?"

"Have you no faith in me at all?"

"Gert, every vacation we've ever taken has been a disaster."

"It must be . . . off-season."

"June?"

"It's clear across the country, John. The seasons are different."

"And you're going to educate *me* on climate change." He snapped the paper back open. "The answer is no."

"But John, it's the perfect romantic getaway."

"What's that have to do with us?"

So, it had come to this. Her husband's edification was in service to the greater good. She had to remember that. Progress could be a game-changer, she thought they called it. Knowing that in war both sides suffer losses, she steeled herself for the pangs of compromise. But the words left a bitter taste.

"There's a golf course."

# # #

The doorbell rang; Al Gore presiding. From elsewhere came the disembodied male voice.

"Bring 'em in through the garage, Gert."

She hurried in from the kitchen as he came hurtling down the steps. She won the race to the door, and welcomed the Padillas with open arms and a big—

"Hello!"

A cute couple, Rodolfo was a slight, introspective man, with a mustache and pleasant smile; Maria cute and vivacious, a little plump. John went blank at the sight of the raven-haired, dark-eyed, white-toothed luminescence that was Victoria.

Gert gave Maria a warm hug. "Welcome to our home, Maria." Rodolfo smiled as Gert took his hand in hers. "And welcome, Rodolfo. It's wonderful to see you again."

"Thank you so much for having us," said Maria. "I hope you don't mind if we brought our daughter, Victoria."

Gert took Victoria's hand. "Of course not. Victoria is welcome."

Victoria smiled self-consciously as her mother went on. "Victoria is home from college on spring break. She's on the dean's list, and we're so proud of her."

"Well, Victoria certainly is a lovely young woman. Maria, I'd like for you to meet my husband, John."

John was gaga. He took Victoria's hand in his. "And your name would be?"

"Uh . . . Victoria." Bemused, she made careful study of her area of the floor.

"I think we've already established her name, John."

"Oh. Haha." He was blushing like a schoolboy.

"Wouldn't you like to meet Maria and Rodolfo?"

"Yes, of course." He shook their hands. "How do you do?"

Maria smiled, noticing the portrait. "Ah, Señor Gore."

"Yes, we're great admirers. John insisted we place it here, in the entrance to our home."

John couldn't take his eyes off that blessing of creation—his pitiful simper fixed in place. Whatever ole whatshername had said, doubtless of little consequence.

"So, how are you, Maria? Are you getting settled in?"

"Yes, we are, Bert, but we're exhausted."

Gert laughed. "It's *Gert*, Maria."

Maria covered her mouth in embarrassment. "Ooh, so sorry."

"That's perfectly alright, Maria. People make that mistake all the time."

There followed an uncomfortable silence, before Gert decided on another stab at Spanish.

"*Y su familia?*"

Maria was delighted to have found a Spanish speaker.

"*Ah, mi familia ! . . . Tengo una familia maravilloso ! Mi familia esta en el Acuitzeramo, un pequeno pueblo en el municipio de Tiazazalca en el estado Mexicano de Michoacan. Mi madre y mis tres hermanos y dos hermanas y sus familias siquen viviendo alli, aungue algunos de ellos estan pensando en venir a los Estados Unidos como lo hicimos nosotros. Mi mama es de sesenta y seis anos y ahora tiene dieciocho nietos. Ella es la mujer mas fantastica del mundo. Perdimos a mi padre en un accidente de transporte por carretera hace dos anos. Era un buen papa, salvo que a veces bebia un poco demasiado. Pero, salvo por la tragica perdida de mi papa, mi familia esta feliz y muy bien, y fue tan amable de su parte para pedir por ellos.*"

Her hostess was caught flat-footed.

"Ah . . . bueno."

#   #   #

A man's home may be his castle, but a woman's boudoir, more specifically her *bed,* is her realm. And in the aftermath of disaster, woman can retreat to that perfect security found only under the covers. Time may heal all wounds, but soft sheets speed the process.

Which is where we found Gert on the morning after. Her boorish husband having told her to shake it off, as he put it, before heading for work. He could never be expected to understand. Not only was he a stone-hearted conservative, or libertarian, or whatever he called himself; he was a man.

It would be a day for healing—and chocolate. Emily Upton's latest memoir lay within reach, bookmark stuck on page six, where it had remained for the better part of a month. *Phil and Me.* It was starting out a lot like her last book, the one Gert got for fifty cents at the library. A malign, misogynistic universe was out to get her, which was true enough, but sometimes even the faithful got tired of the whining.

This one she had found for $2.99 on the bargain table at Barnes and Noble. No one she knew had ever paid full retail for any of Emily's books. In truth, she had never been able to finish one. Leslie claimed to have read every one at least twice. How did she do it?

So, there it was. A choice between *Phil and Me,* and the romance novel she'd selected from the same bargain table. She opened *Love After Lockdown*—along with the bag of fun-size Hershey Bars—even as her calm was shattered by the phone call.

"America's a sewer. I agree."

"Blah-bluh-blah?"

"The dinner? Well, it was a little awkward, to say the least."

"Bluh-blah?"

"Yes, they were. From Mexico."

"Blah-blah, blah-bluh-blah-blah."

"I know, my Spanish will never compare to yours, Leslie." She sighed, as she considered her many and varied shortcomings. "And of course, John was a complete embarrassment."

"Blah-bluh-blah."

"I don't know why I put up with him either."

"Bluh-bluh-blah, blah-blah."

"No social graces whatsoever. He spent the entire evening ogling their daughter. Gaping at her through those overgrown eyebrows."

"Bluh-blah?"

"I guess she was pretty." She listened for a moment before bursting into tears. "I'm losing him, Leslie! I keep hoping this trip can revive some of the romance, but all he wants to do is play golf."

"Blah-blah-blah-blah-blah."

"I know he's not much, but he's all I have."

"Blah-bluh-blah-blah. Bluh-blah. Bluh-bluh-blah."

"That's easy for you to say. Brock is a gem. Wherever did you find him?" Brock had gotten his law degree from Columbia, but Gert couldn't remember where he and Leslie had met. "He quotes Shakespeare. And Yeats. And Bertrand Russell. . . . All I ever get from John is this H.L. Mencken."

"Blah-blah-blah."

"You met him at *which* March on Washington?"

Leslie could be domineering, but as she reminisced about happy times with Brock her tone softened. "Of course it's hard, but isn't it worth it?" Gert asked. She pulled a Kleenex from a box on the night table and wiped a last tear. "What's the matter, Leslie?"

"Blah-blah. Bluh-blah-blah. Sniff-sniff."

Gert sat up. "You're crying." She transferred the box of Kleenex to her lap.

"Boo-hoo, blah-blah-blah, boo-hoo."

"But . . . where is he?" She listened in horror. "Two *months*. Leslie, why didn't you . . . ?"

"Boo-hoo. Boo-hoo-hoo-hoo."

Gert pulled another Kleenex for a good blow. "Don't cry, Leslie. You'll get him back."

CHAPTER 4

Stacy and Friends

In the weeks leading up to takeoff, primary season heated up. Riding high on bluster and his war hero reputation, Jim O'Leary dispensed with his Republican rivals and turned his attention to the Democrats. As serious issues facing everyday Americans were drowned out by the social justice cacophony, no smart politician dared stray from party-approved talking points for fear of alienating any recognized or nascent victim group. Our vulnerable communities. One of the largest, and therefore most valuable as political currency, the twenty million or so who, under the nose of the bureaucracy, and with the blessing of the controlling class, had stolen into the land of the free in search of opportunity; but would settle for free education and health care. Only in twenty-first century America, as John phrased it, could a foreign national and his family sneak into someone else's country—and bring along a list of demands. Her husband heartless, according to his wife, to even think of a humanitarian crisis along such hard-bitten lines.

The few actual policy statements made largely concerned pecuniary transfers, from the productive to the non, drafted with the utmost, focus-group driven care. Strategies devised by campaign brains for separating Tweedledee from Tweedledum centered on contrived differences between three candidates who had already sold their souls to establishment power brokers, and stood poised to pander to any and all. Opinion polls generally favored the candidate promising the most goodies.

Character assassinations ran the gamut. Scandal opened on the coasts; and came soon to the Peorias, and a theater near you. Crafted out of whole cloth, the better to protect the guilty. Sex and lucre abounded in Washington, but it was understood by the players that *personal* matters were out of bounds, and best kept between friends. Exhaustive security files maintained by our honorable intelligence community (thanks to assets like the late Jeffrey Epstein), protected deep-state interests against any who might get too frisky. Reprisals could be hell. Confidentiality was Washington's sole remaining virtue.

The underpinnings of politics is falsehood. Pledge transparency, but keep the masses in the dark. Truth is a dangerous thing in the wrong hands. Likewise, dissent in the ranks. The game goes on—clock turned off—as long as everyone plays by the rules. The chance malcontent is a source of irritation, but there are countermeasures. Even the most scurrilous lie could be validated by *New York Times/Washington Post* consensus. From seed came rumor; rumor leading to accusation; accusation established as fact on the word of anonymous sources. Others would learn from his example.

Only the sapient bothered to notice the metamorphosis of the networks from news outlets, to propaganda arms. A century of indoctrination over education in the public schools—thank you, John Dewey, Edward Bernays, et al.—to go with stultifying entertainment, had divested America of its last vestige of cognitive function, or even the need to know.

Blind faith in permanent Washington, or regard for the drivel streaming from the ivory towers of academe, marked one as well informed. Those who dared question representing a clear and present danger. You were *alt* this, or that; by whatever means, silenced. The controllers prey on existing fears, while conjuring new ones. Keep the people off balance. Fear and uncertainty clear the way for *mass formation psychosis*—and the imposition of virtually any form of official horror. When the elemental human need for security is satisfied, the hungry masses line up to feed. From Machiavelli to Pelosi, the formula has remained the same. Trade reason for *feeling*. The information age had given way to the *emotion age* in the seduction of gelded minds.

Social media was the dirty bomb of a new era; race the yellowcake. Low information me-centric voters are notoriously suggestible. A respected voice can lend legitimacy to the latest charges brought against one due for a fall, or disclose *dramatic new developments*; CNN and MSNBC pile on; and by the middle of the next morning Jane and John Q. Public were convinced they'd known it all along.

Though she and her sisters carried their own victim banner high, even one as practiced in the art as Emily Upton had to tread lightly in her criticism of Benjamin Jamaal Singh for fear of being labeled a racist. The R word was certain death for any candidate; all it took was one slip. The best defense being a good offense, she loaded her campaign with African Americans; from her campaign chairman and legal team, all the way down to precinct workers. Menial tasks such as going for coffee, sweeping up after rallies (which Democrats rarely did anyway), and taking out the trash delegated exclusively to the odd white male. If only she could dump that worthless white husband of hers, but he would be needed. For whatever reason, America still loved him.

It was one of those open Washington secrets that the Emily campaign was looking for dirt they could hang on Jim O'Leary. If they could somehow paint *him* as a racist, it could only help her in the race against Jamaal Singh; and should she win the nomination, make her a virtual shoo-in come November. This would take some doing, for Jim O'Leary had always been regarded as a champion of civil rights. He'd been a principal sponsor of the Voting Rights Act, and for years favored blanket amnesty for illegal aliens; his opponents on the Right accusing the maverick senator of being open borders.

Here again, the Emily campaign had to watch its step. Though questions remained as to the veracity of O'Leary's claimed hero status, every member of today's glorified military, retired or active, was automatically a hero, even had he never seen duty beyond a desk stateside. The uniform entitled the wearer to a catalog of benefits, ranging from free meals at the local Taco Bell, to Super Bowl tickets. Thank you for your service to our country, and all that. And besides, the Pentagon owned Washington. On the other hand, as everyone knows, servicemen speak their own colorful language, and the guy was from Texas for crying out loud—the land of God, guns, and good ole boys. There had to be something.

John watched the parody play out nightly from the vantage of his recliner. He knew from four Washington decades that there was not a dime's bit of difference between the two parties, or the three candidates. They were owned up to their earlobes. The fun would be watching to see which of three clunkers won the favor of the powers backstage, and hence, the presidency.

Though the decisions taken by the networks on which candidate to favor came from the top, that didn't necessarily dissuade newsroom liberals, schooled in acceptable thinking, from having their own biases. Or discreet operatives from the Upton campaign dipping into petty cash to assist a few up-and-coming journalists with their rent; the cost of living being what it was in Washington. It was a natural assumption that Emily Upton would be the favorite of women in the media. From CNN's

Washington Bureau, it had been leaked that certain reporters were investigating claims that Jim O'Leary may, on at least one occasion, have uttered a racial slur back in high school.

It made no difference whether or not it really happened. Or that Emily Upton's closed-door lexicon was known to be sufficiently raw, to say nothing of racially peppered, to make prison inmates wince. That was just Emily being Emily. All that would be required for Operation R to succeed would be for a couple of tearful former classmates to come forward and testify that they had been scarred for life by their young classmate's vile epithets. Vehement denials notwithstanding, any white male Republican would be presumed guilty. And no matter how flimsy the evidence, by the time an impartial jury of journalists was done with him, any exoneration would smell of cover-up.

Alas, the mission failed to launch. Perusal of his high school yearbooks by Fox News revealed a number of pictures of a young Jim O'Leary in the company of a pretty African American girl named, ironically, Angela White. The two had dated each other almost exclusively during his junior and senior years; over the objections of *both* sets of parents.

Oops. Reached at her Tucson, Arizona home, the now 72-year-old Angela Perkins, née White, fondly remembered young Jim O'Leary as the sweetest boy she had ever known. His notorious womanizing having begun sometime thereafter. Operation R was scuttled, and for Emily and her dirty tricksters, it was back to the well.

Meanwhile, Benjamin Jamaal Singh was racking up primary wins. The media mavens decided to play the Democratic race down the middle—a contest between the would-be first woman, or the first Jewish/African/ formerly Muslim/Hindu American president a no-win pick in the identity derby. The candidates would be left to their own resources, with the DC press corps confident Emily still had a few up her pantsuit.

Things were looking bleak until her big win in California, where she drew upon guilt sewn by the state's two female senators. Standing before her *STRONGER DIVERSE!* banner, she addressed her supporters.

"I'd like to take this opportunity to congratulate my worthy opponent on a hard-fought race here in the Golden State," she rasped. After an equally hard-fought win over her hacking cough, she was able to squeak breathlessly, "But the people of California have spo—(cough, cough)—ken. Thank you, Cali—(cough, cough, cough)—fornia!" For no visible reason she erupted into laughter, gleefully singling out total strangers in the crowd.

It was looking like a contested convention.

#   #   #

They were on the first of the scheduled flights that would eventually land them close enough for the final overland leg to the remote village of Progress, Oregon. Gert had the window seat, whining to her husband about being cramped. He was in the middle. In the aisle seat, a four-hundred-pound hulk was overtly violating John's space. As the man slept, the situation was assessed in whispers.

"The guy is hogging the armrest."

"He's asleep."

"And look. His foot is on my side, and his whole leg is spilling over."

"Your white privilege is showing. It would be rude of you to wake him."

"What does my color have to do with this, pray tell?"

"Your sense of entitlement, John," punctuated by a peevish sigh. "You don't even realize . . ."

"He's white too, in case you hadn't noticed." He longed for the happy bygone days of gracious air travel.

"You're an elitist, John. Always quick to *other*. You and your sort."

Three flight attendants as plain as doorknobs patrolled the aisles with their little handhelds, debiting passengers' accounts for everything but oxygen. John remembered a day when complimentary food and beverage were served with a smile by pretty stewardesses wearing dresses.

"If it were an attractive *woman* you wouldn't object."

How did she do that? "If it were an attractive woman, she could sit in my lap."

"You're a dirty old man. And I haven't forgotten that night with the Padillas. You had better watch yourself on this trip."

"So I'm supposed to just sit like this the entire flight. I can barely breathe."

"The poor man cannot be held responsible for what he does in his sleep. He's already been marginalized by impolite society on account of his size, and it would be sadistic on your part to call further attention to it. The man is suffering, John!"

John looked to his left. His neighbor in dreamland.

"He's not suffering now."

"You have an unconscious bias against large people. I've seen it."

He rested back in his seat, blank gaze toward the ceiling, and Heaven above. "Help me."

"Sir, please return your seat to the upright position," he was admonished.

Gert was rereading *Earth in The Balance* by Al Gore; remembering, with a tingle, her first time.

"You know, virtually everything in that book has been debunked."

"The book is two decades old, John. Of course there have been new findings."

"You mean like finding it all amounts to penguin droppings."

"Now you're an authority on climate science."

"I know the author's a con artist, who's gotten very rich crisscrossing the globe by private jet."

He picked up his *Washington Times*. Prominent on page one were two headlines: "O'Leary Slams Special Interests" and "Jamaal Singh Says O'Leary Caters to Special Interests." Lambent inspiration played in blue eyes.

"So, did Brock leave Leslie for a man or a woman?"

"That's not the least bit funny, John." She put down her book. "If you must know, he's moved in with some floozy from the Heritage Foundation. He's eating meat . . . and everything."

"Speaking ill of a sister?"

"Laugh all you want."

He threw back his head and did.

"You're creating a scene."

"Good ole Brock."

"At least Leslie stands for something. You just hate everything."

"I like Jon Small."

Jon Small was the insurgent congressman from Louisiana who had dared to defy the established order. He'd entered the presidential race as a long shot, but was generating a lot of excitement, especially among disenfranchised younger voters who liked his libertarian views. He was opposed to military intervention overseas, advocated a balanced budget, and limited constitutional government. In his boldest proposal, he called for the abolishment of the Federal Reserve System, the private consortium of unaccountable big shots that set monetary policy, and printed paper dollars at will. Ridiculed by press potentates as out of touch, it hadn't stopped followers from flocking to his rallies by the thousand.

"The one that everybody laughs at."

"Behind closed doors they're not laughing. The keepers of the status quo are scared to death by an honest man."

"He wants to do away with the EPA. He'd put you out of a job, John."

"Give me time to form my think tank."

"You're talking nonsense."

He thought he had won that round, she was sure. But his ideas were old and tired, and he thought he could make points by joking about every-thing. The planet was in peril thanks to her husband and his ilk, laughing their way to doomsday. This was a battle we couldn't afford to lose.

"Airline travel is so wasteful," she averred, as she studied cloud formations.

He knew she was talking energy stores and carbon footprints, but he wasn't playing ball. "Flying from Baltimore to Atlanta, by way of Cincinnati? On our way to Oregon? I guess you could say that."

"We should take the train next time. That's how Europeans travel."

"I'm sure they know best."

She abruptly began brushing the shoulder of his navy blue shirt.

"Your dandruff is back."

# # #

She guessed they were somewhere over Kentucky or Tennessee, on their way to Atlanta. If there was one thing, she knew her geography. Which were the green states, which the polluters. John did have a point. It didn't make much sense flying in the wrong direction, but that was the airlines.

She looked over at her husband, sound asleep. Some companion. At least he wasn't one of those people who slept with their mouth hanging open. That would have been so embarrassing.

He wasn't snoring, but now he was mumbling something about "the women." This, reason for not the slightest concern on her part. Horny as he was, Gert knew her husband would not be doing any Diego Rivera number on her. Cheating without getting caught was work. John was lazy.

She remembered the young man of promise. She had always been proud of the way he made her friends laugh. And he was so cute with his beard and ponytail. Proud activist (or so he made out), he looked the part. What might he have been? She couldn't recall him ever having any career aspirations, though. Most of the guys at school had wanted to be *something*. Mostly, John liked to drink, or get high. He ate, and had sex, and slept. He did read a lot, and he'd always loved baseball. In the heat of a pennant race, she got used to making love while he kept one eye on the game. He wasn't really a party animal. He would just get slowly wasted, a fixture at his corner table in The Vous, regaling the motley muddled with his observations. Dispensing movie and music reviews. His Tony Kubek impressions. Everyone always talked about how smart he was, but she didn't see it. He managed to graduate without going to class much. She asked him once if he cheated, and he said he was good at taking multiple-choice tests. Generally, only two choices being viable, he could usually spot the trick answer. Turning in written work had been a problem. In those early days of grade inflation he could turn the 1.8 he deserved, into a 2.8, by schmoozing the female instructors, or doing a snow job on the males. Feigning a higher intellectual plane. He talked a lot about intellectual planes.

Looking back, she believed he fancied himself the group's thinker. He *had* his following. He probably would have been content as sage in a commune somewhere, but she remembered the promise he made to her father to support her. Her mother said John was shiftless. John had said that was kind of true, but it was more that he was just mellow.

She wasn't sure now how much his heart had been in their various causes. He maybe went along just to make her happy. A lot of the guys were like that, probably. Guys were pigs. Not beyond anything that could get them laid. Planning sessions consisted of John and the other young lions sitting around getting high, while the girls did everything.

Brainstorming, they called it. There was always plenty of weed to go around in those days, but she couldn't recall any occasion on which John had made a contribution.

In that sexually liberated circle he had been pretty faithful. Now and then, though, he might disappear for a while; and later she would remember that one of her friends had been gone around the same time. The rat. At least he never gave her anything.

Until the time when, in the middle of his Mel Allen, he was summarily informed that the second test had also come back positive. The bum then had the balls to ask if she was sure it was his. A surgical strike to his nearest knee served for an answer. Knowing him as she did, she had made a point of wearing her boots.

No problem, Leslie and her friends said. Roe vs. Wade had set them free. And there were already clinics in DC.

But the thought made her sick to her stomach. In addition to the morning sickness she was already experiencing. She believed wholeheartedly in a woman's right to choose. But not in her case. She already loved that little life growing inside of her.

And then a strange and wonderful thing happened. Her knight in shining armor had ridden to the rescue. No one was doing any such thing, to any son of *his*, he informed that collection of losers.

It probably came at an opportune time. They were set to graduate. She had figured on eventually marrying John; there didn't seem to be anyone else around. And she was beginning to think she might actually love him. All the other girls did. But he hadn't seemed in any hurry, and she wasn't sure he even believed in marriage.

But for the sake of his mother, and her father, he decided to do the bourgeois thing and make it legal. The very same "friends," who two weeks earlier had encouraged her to vacuum the unwelcome *it* from her womb, filled the campus chapel to share in her joy.

# # #

She didn't know why he was so grumpy. He had grown rather impatient over the years. He knew going in that they would be making connections. They were delayed for forty-five minutes in Atlanta, but were still scheduled to make it to Salt Lake City in plenty of time for their connecting flight to Portland.

"Why can't we just fly to Portland?"

"Because Salt Lake City is a hub, John." She wasn't exactly sure what that meant, but it sounded like something she had heard.

"I thought Atlanta was a hub."

"I . . . think it is."

"How many hubs are there?"

Their seats were in the next to last row. Gert waited for him to take the middle, but her husband was making a rare stand. "My boarding pass says that I"—index finger explicitly indicating his person—"have the aisle seat."

"You know I can't be in the middle seat."

He stowed their carry-ons, and plopped down in the middle. "Which is fine. I *love* the middle seat."

"Maybe you should order a drink, John. It would improve your disposition."

The cabin door was shut, and safety instructions were being given. The young girl in the window seat was walled off by her phone—doing obeisance at the 5G altar. She had slid the shade down so the two of them could be alone. All around him they were lowered. This was a recent phenomenon. A little power trip by those in the window seats maybe? Americans feeling powerless generally, this was their chance at a day in the sun. Or out of it. They would decide who saw what. For John, there was the sensation of traveling by submarine at forty thousand feet. Given his choice, he would have preferred snow-capped mountain vistas, deep blue lakes, mighty cities, and green geometry; to the empty stares of dull people. A generation raised on *Star Wars*.

Had we lost our sense of wonder? Curiosity even? GPS at their fingertips, the phone drones phound their way through the phog, blissfully unconscious of their surroundings, or even where they might find themselves; knowing only that with help from space they had somehow made it there. This applied, it would seem, to the whole of the planet. Had *experience* come to be defined in terms of what was playing on one's screen when something real happened? All part of the terrain in being hip, John guessed, in a media-fueled climate of righteous self-aggrandizement. They'd flown before. It was no big deal.

The baby behind them was starting to cry. The know-it-all with the New York accent, who hadn't stopped talking since they boarded, forced to raise his voice to be heard. For whatever reason, the baby's father couldn't stop sneezing. Someone in proximity, phonephace most likely, was subsisting on garlic alone. Gert took out her latest *Mother Jones* and glanced over at John, hands folded politely in his lap.

"Why don't you read that book you just bought?"

"I would love to read the book I just bought."

"Well then, why don't you?"

"Because I left it in the restaurant."

# # #

It was some of the worst turbulence they had ever experienced, and she was sure he would find a way to blame her. They were literally bouncing in their seats. The baby, whose parents had started bickering on takeoff, was shrieking, and the New Yorker was explaining that there was no cause for alarm because planes were built to withstand that kind of punishment.

Four rows up, a young girl in the throes of panic was being attended by a pair of physicians fortunate to be on board. The right wing was about to break off! Couldn't they *see* that?

John listened to the pilot's latest warning—the eleventh by his count—that they should remain in their seats, with belts securely fastened. Passengers contended with flight attendants, arguing that they had *to go*. Whoever was playing that annoying hip-hop kept turning it up louder and louder. And it was so cold in the cabin, John was sure someone must have left a window open. None of which was helping a bad case of heartburn. He half wondered if it might be for the best if it all ended right there.

# # #

It had been a rough landing, but now they were safely in Salt Lake City. There was just enough time for John to repurchase his book, and make it to their gate. As he read the introduction to *The Truth About Identity Politics*, Gert looked disdainfully his way.

"What exactly do they mean by identity politics?"

"Divide and conquer. The oldest trick in the tyrant playbook."

The faces not in phones were blank. Were people this bored, or was it just cool to be blasé? He wasn't bored. He was ready to go home.

"So, what's so special about this Progress, Oregon?"

She was instantly buoyed by that glimmer of interest. "I'm glad you finally asked, John. Progress, Oregon, is a vivid canvas of Nature in all Her splendor! Towering pines that run all the way to the blue Pacific; waves crashing on the rocky shoreline; sea lions in their native habitat. All the wonders of Nature, unspoiled by man." She shone with evangelistic fervor.

Pulled from a future dystopia, the canned female voice was warning them about leaving bags unattended. As if a madman lurked around every corner, lethal gizmo concealed under his raincoat, timer set, waiting for just the right moment. Had anyone, foreign or domestic, of any religion, ever been known to have inserted any weapon, of any kind, into any stranger's bag, in *any* American airport? The ominous alert played every ninety seconds, wary passengers glancing anxiously from side to side, carry-ons pressed to breasts. One cannot be too careful.

Which brought to mind the whole charade, currently enjoying a twenty-year run in the security theater of the absurd. With all of the technology, the lines, the pat-downs, and the dirty looks from supercilious high school dropouts; to the millions of toiletries expropriated, and *billions* of shoes removed, had there ever been, in the history of the TSA, a single apprehension of even *one* honest-to-God terrorist? Big Brother tending his flock, while his extended family rakes in unseemly profits playing on the fears, and enduring patience, of sheep. Pardon John his cynicism.

There was one of his favorite airport characters: the traveling executive. Impressive in bearing. Flying first-class no doubt, business casual in tailored dress shirt, crisp collar open at the neck, five-hundred dollar Italian loafers, and . . . jeans? *Designer* jeans, at that? A more ludicrous ensemble would be hard to imagine, and yet John saw it every time he flew. Whom did these fifty- and sixty-somethings think they were kidding?

Gert noticed him too, and her heart leaped. He was handsome, and so stylish. And there was John to her right. She was picturing the magnificent home where this gentleman must live, when she caught herself. *He* was the patriarchy. How could she, even if only for an unguarded moment, have forgotten the crimes of the one percent?

But that didn't excuse her sorry sight of a husband. With the scraggly hair he insisted on cutting himself because he was too cheap. All slouched, sartorial pileup in the usual wrinkled khakis, and that blue golf shirt. She couldn't believe it wasn't a rag by now. The moth-eaten New Balance—was that a hole in the *other* toe?—heels ground to mirror angles of forty-five degrees. How did he even walk in those things?

With ten minutes to boarding John did a quick survey. Every eye, to include those of his wife, was fixed on some screen. The Smiths of Silver Spring could waltz naked the length of Terminal C, and pass virtually unnoticed. But every so often the devil's playground served a legitimate purpose.

"What did the Orioles do?"

Real-time data was retrieved instantaneously. "They won."

Yes. The Yankees were in town the following week, and he had tickets.

"Millie has a new doctor, a Dr. Grimsley," said Gert, eyes never straying from her device. "He says she's a classic case of histrionic personality disorder." The preceding was noted with raised eyebrow.

"Never heard of it."

"Maybe it's something new."

"Then how can her case be classic?"

"It's characterized by an overwhelming need for attention."

"Is gin the recommended therapy?"

Behind them, a woman, her white hair dyed a lurid *off*-white, was giving her elderly husband a public flogging for losing their boarding passes. "It took me thirty minutes with that air-headed little airline person to get the situation straightened out, Henry. You do this all the time. Why are you always so forgetful? Careless and forgetful."

Henry offered no defense.

"You're a hopeless case. I'm your wife, but sometimes I feel more like your babysitter. You need to be more responsible, Henry." On it went.

John turned to Gert. "She could give you lessons."

"Quiet, John," she whispered. "They can hear you."

So strong were this latter-day Agrippina's convictions regarding this flawed man, and her own noble forbearance, that she was not to be deterred. She searched the faces of their fellow fliers, gauging the level of her support, before starting back in. Poor Henry was either hard of hearing, or suffering a slow and painful death in quiet dignity.

Having heard enough, John struck a blow for underappreciated husbands everywhere. "Our friend Henry, here, in all likelihood supported this old bag for her entire adult life. And now listen."

Exposed, his target pretended not to hear—her fresh silence evidence she had.

"I'm glad you said that," pronounced the woman sitting to John's right.

Not a moment too soon came the announcement: "Now boarding, Flight 213, nonstop service to Portland."

"I should certainly hope," said John, making sure to remember his book.

# # #

Her winged name tag identified her as one Stacy Smart. A no-nonsense redhead who was evidently having a rough night. John and Gert waited at her counter at the Portland International Airport as she studied her computer monitor.

"The name is Smith," said the weary travelers in unison.

"Can you spell that?"

"It's spelled like *Smith*," said John.

"That was a serious question, sir," said she in the dark blue blazer, refusing to crack a smile. "Impertinent passengers, Mr. Smith, can find themselves on the No-Fly List. Okay, I've got it. John and Gertrude."

She typed for an interminable length of time. How did she go so fast without messing up? And what was she typing?

"I see the problem. You're one boarding pass short." Scroll and click. "Your next stop is *Eugene*, and from there you take a connecting flight to Coos Bay."

"You're kidding," John blurted. He checked his watch.

"Do I look like I'm kidding?"

"What did you expect for this price, John? You are the most impatient man I've ever known."

The ticket agent's phone rang. She answered with a friendly skies smile. "Good evening, Midwest Airways." She listened, smile dissipating. "Kevin, you have to be firm with them. You tell them that if they're not washed and in bed before Mommy gets home, there will be hell to pay!" She slammed the receiver.

"How did this happen?" Gert asked bravely.

Stacy Smart looked her right in the eye. "How should I know?"

"Six flights? They probably lost count."

"I don't know that I appreciate your sarcasm, John." She was starting to cry. "I worked hard putting this trip together."

"Multnomah Air only flies as far as Eugene. From there, you'll be taking a single-engine charter, leased by Pioneer Express, for your forty-five-minute flight to Coos Bay."

Blue golf shirt groaned.

"It was a *package*, John."

She handed them two Multnomah Air boarding passes. Changed screens. "Now, as to the whereabouts of your golf clubs." She studied her data. "According to what I have here, they are currently in . . . Or-*lan*-do. The good news is that we should be able to get them to you in a day or two via bonded courier. At absolutely no cost to you!" Delivered with a sub-zero smile.

"That's most generous."

Stacy Smart knew sarcasm when she heard it, but there was little left to say in this transcontinental showdown.

And John didn't dare cross her. His prized possession was in the hands of strangers, *she* had the key, and he couldn't run the risk of missing out on this kind of fun in the future.

"Boarding is in one hour at gate B-19."

An hour?

# # #

There is a sameness to airport men's rooms. They are uniformly immaculate, tourism being a vital sector of the service economy, and each city endeavoring to put its best foot forward.

Sustainability paramount in an age of climate flux, the Portland airport, like its brethren, sounded a familiar note on a common theme: the hygienic receptacle/washbasin dichotomy. No doubt higher in the pecking order, and rightly so, the receptacle, be it semiprivate commode or more public urinal, by necessity responds powerfully on command, the conservation of crystal clear water no barrier to performance. Be advised to keep hands and feet clear.

The conveniences we take for granted. A giant step forward, the urinal. As John backed away, it flushed automatically, and his thoughts drifted thousands of miles to his personal favorite: one in his office men's room. The one he invariably chose over its unremarkable partner. The fixture fascinated him. It drained poorly, and when flushed would fill to within a quarter inch of the rim. And no further. It was diabolical, as if a mysterious sensor secreted deep within the porcelain saw to the perfect flow. With each flush, he would hold his breath—girding for that call to housekeeping—but it had yet to fail him. The Do Not Use! sign held in abeyance another day.

It was at the row of sinks where technology and sustainability collided, rendering the simple act of washing one's hands an endurance test for the modern traveler. Faucet sensors a 50/50 proposition at best, it generally took multiple passes before one struck water, with the average three-second squirt barely sufficient to dampen sullied hands. Subsequent attempts proving futile, it was on to a neighbor for another feeble shot. From there, to contend with towel dispensers gone digital; soapy hands performing a variety of yoga moves, before being wiped on pants.

# # #

Gert had decided to have her nails done, and John figured the beer in the terminal would be cheaper than that on the plane. The TV in the bar was tuned to CNN, where Emily Upton sat for a heart-to-heart with Sarah Mills, sounding off on the perils of running for president in a man's world. She began the interview calmly and evenly; the carnage that was to follow largely self-inflicted. With John enjoying every minute of a painful performance.

"This campaign isn't about me, Sarah," said Emily in earnest. "It's about empowering women. It's been an uphill slog my whole life," she said between coughs. "You've experienced it. It's time we had a serious conversation about sexism in this country. We all know about the glass ceiling. Now I'm hearing reports that Jim O'Leary is questioning the effectiveness of women in combat. Rehashing all of the tired old arguments about it being damaging to unit cohesion, that women can't pull their weight, the rash of pregnancies, and so on and so forth. All proven categorically untrue."

By whom? When? John wanted data.

"What about the argument that the military is not the place for a government-run social experiment?" Mills asked.

Emily cut loose with her famous cackle. "Sarah, we all know that right-wing trope is simply dog-whistle sexism. As long as insecure men are intimidated by strong women, we're going to continue to hear these lame excuses for keeping us down."

"Do you think Jim O'Leary is intimidated by you?" This prompted another grating cackle, from one who had never given the world any other indication she *had* a sense of humor.

"Maybe, just maybe, this war hero is afraid of a strong woman. Proving my point!" she concluded, index finger thrust in the air.

"You scare the hell out of me, lady," John was forced to admit.

"And you've certainly had to face other forms of discrimination," continued Mills, *muy* simpatico. "We've even had Benjamin Jamaal Singh, caught on a live mic, joking that your preference for pantsuits is because you have legs, I believe he put it, like tree trunks. For the record, he has apologized."

Was that really a tear? Oh, brother.

"It's a shame, Sarah. Even my worthy opponent for the Democratic nomination, a good progressive, has stooped to making jokes about my physical appearance and wardrobe choices. I wouldn't be subjected to such personal attacks if I was a man."

"With Jim O'Leary, on more than one occasion, referring to you as an empty pantsuit."

"Jim O'Leary's a fine one to talk. Finishing third from the bottom in his class at West Point."

Score one for Emily. But even from his seat, John could see the cheeks trending crimson, puffy eyes aflame.

"And then you have white privilege Fox News with their over-the-top conspiracy theories about me and my husband, and the work of our foundation. It's just scandalous."

Interesting choice of words, John thought.

"I know it's a delicate issue, but speaking of your husband—"

"Oh, please, Sarah, don't you start."

"Well, there have been reports . . ."

"Lies, Sarah. All lies. You see, this is what I'm talking about. A woman makes for an easy target. Men don't get asked these questions. Why don't you ask Jim O'Leary about his first marriage? Because he's a man, that's why. Or Benjamin Jamaal Singh about the rumors that he was really born on Cyprus. Why? Because the reporters are afraid of being labeled racist. Not that I'm a racist, mind you. And anyway, why should I have to come on here and defend myself? I'll put my civil rights record up against anybody's."

"And then there is what is referred to as your storied temper . . ."

"Why aren't I forty points ahead? you might ask," she fumed in answer. "This is why! It's the same old story, Sarah. Questions about my health," she coughed, "or my temperament. Or whether or not I've had a facelift, or how I wear my hair. No one talks about Jim O'Leary's transplants. I ask you, Sarah, what do any of these things have to do with being commander in chief? The vicious rumors about my family and my personal life. And women voting against me because their husbands tell them to. The old boys club ganging up on the girl."

Poor Emily.

CHAPTER 5

Mrs. Gilroy

In the dead of night, they waited. With two huge bags, two medium, and two carry-ons. Behind them, the security officer locked the front entrance to the Coos Bay Airport. They had been the lone passengers on the last arriving flight.

Gert broke the silence. "The Eugene airport was lovely. I can't say as much for this place."

That was the least of his concerns. "Five bags?"

"They have wheels, John."

After a check of his watch, "You sure the guy's coming?"

"He said twenty minutes."

"It's already been thirty."

"What time is it?" she was almost afraid to ask.

"Eleven-fifty. Pacific."

The security officer gave them a wave as he sped off, leaving them alone with the two sleeping vagrants, and row of light aircraft on the other side of the chain-link fence. Knowing the mood he was in, she opted for empathy. "We've been up for twenty-one hours."

"Twenty-four."

At least the final two flights had been uneventful. The last pilot was very nice, chatty even, up to the point where John asked that he please keep his eye on the sky. He just hadn't cared for the gentleman's politics. That was it. She grinned to herself. In Progress, John would be in over his head. She didn't like to see her husband humiliated, but he was due for a comeuppance.

The cab arrived.

"Finally."

"Patience, John."

Gert climbed in the back, as the cabbie hopped out and hustled around to get their bags. When he struggled with the large bags, John gave him an assist. "What's your wife got in these bags?"

Inside, the picture matched their driver, so the cabbie's name was Milton. "Good evening, Milton," said Gert.

"Actually, it's morning, Mrs. Smith."

"Yes, Milton, I guess you're right about that. It is my sincere pleasure. I was afraid we wouldn't be meeting many African Americans."

"Well, it's my pleasure to exceed your expectations, Mrs. Smith."

John was an exhausted heap, with neither the inclination to speak, nor the energy necessary.

"How far is it to Progress?" Gert inquired, her cheerfulness wearing thin on her husband. He was good and grumpy, and he planned on staying that way.

"Oh, about twenty-five minutes."

John closed suffering eyes and shook his weary head.

"That's if we don't make any wrong turns. I get kinda confused on the roads around there, and they ain't on the GPS."

"Be quiet and let the man concentrate, Gert."

"So, this is your first trip to Progress, I take it?"

"Yes, it is!" Gert piped.

"Why?" asked John.

"Oh," Milton demurred, "no reason."

# # #

After driving around in circles for an extra twenty minutes, they came to a stop at an isolated outpost, enshrouded in the night shadow of looming pines. The headlights illuminated the massive sign: WELCOME TO PROGRESS! NORTH AMERICA'S PROGRESSIVE VACATION DESTINATION! *A Proud Sanctuary City.* Non-motorized vehicles only. Please.

Beyond the presence of the sign, there was nothing to distinguish between that spot—and the middle of nowhere.

"We're here!" Gert gushed.

"Where?" John asked.

"There's no motorized vehicles allowed inside borough limits," said Milton. "They make too much carbon, or something."

He turned off the headlights. The interior light went off as they closed their doors—only to be swallowed by an opaque nothingness. They felt their way around to the back of the cab.

"Ow! You stepped on my toe, John."

It served her right. But—"Can't you at least leave the headlights on?"—seemed a reasonable question.

"Mrs. Gilroy says it spooks the wildlife," replied the local. There was light again as he popped the trunk.

"Who is this Mrs. Gilroy?"

"You'll find out."

"How do we get there from here?" John asked, not sure he wanted to know.

Milton chuckled. "You're gonna have to *walk*."

"Oh, dear." The website had not included this little footnote.

"They have a bike shuttle, but it don't run after dark." They scraped the bags out of the trunk. "You people brought a lotta stuff."

"How far is it?"

"Don't worry. It looks farther—but it's less than two miles."

"Two *miles*."

"Keep your voice down, John. The wildlife."

He switched to a high-decibel rasp. "We've gotta lug these things two miles?"

"It's not *quite* two miles," Milton assured him.

"They have wheels, John."

"Sometimes they have carts you can take," he said, looking around, "but I don't see one." He slammed the trunk shut, leaving them again in the dark. "Your eyes will adjust." He sounded so positive.

"Just be glad they lost your clubs," Gert added, sounding a helpful note.

Milton was happy to direct. "What you do is, you follow this dirt road . . . See that faint glow?"

# # #

Gert held the door for John as he struggled with their bags, medium riding atop the large. She supplied a steadying hand as he tugged the combinations through the door.

"Gee, thanks."

"Oh, stop whining."

"I'm not whining. I'm grousing."

"Where's your sense of adventure?"

The lobby of The Progress Inn was warmly lit and inviting. A woman's cheery voice greeted them from the back room. "We've been waiting for you."

On the wall the big hand was on the six, little hand halfway past the one. The redoubtable Mrs. Gilroy burst from the back room in her combination scurry/waddle, and took up her position behind the desk. She was pleasingly plump, and though of like age, looked years younger than her guests. Tight gray curls framed a jolly face, with eyes that smiled brightly on the outside. Gert had read so much about this internet luminary, that she knew this had to be her.

"You must have had a most exciting trip. May I help you with those bags?"

John was dragging the bags to the desk. Gert followed, favoring her side with the damaged toe.

"He's fine."

As John leaned his weight into the desk, his depleted state was not lost on the proprietress. "You look like you've had a long day."

"A wheel broke on one of the bags, so John had to drag that one."

"But isn't it a lovely walk?"

"At one o'clock in the morning?" This was her alright.

"I'm afraid John is not the most patient man."

"Well, that's all very nice. Welcome to The Progress Inn. I'm Mrs. Gilroy, keeper of the inn, and mayor of the Borough of Progress. A safe space for all."

"It is indeed an honor to make your acquaintance, Mrs. Gilroy." For this visitor it bordered on hero worship. Here was a woman living her dream. It was only one small corner of the world, but in that progressive Elysium more lives were being touched than a Mrs. Gilroy could ever imagine. And she left her mark on people's hearts, not the environment.

There was a rustic look and feel to the lobby, like that of a mountain lodge, with its rough-hewn timbers and beams. Behind the desk hung a painting of a majestic Oregon mountainscape. As Mrs. Gilroy worked at the computer, John did a survey, senses deployed. Was that a musty scent? Not overpowering, certainly, but it was there. He wandered from the desk, and in desultory fashion moved about the room, on the prowl for other indications of subpar housekeeping. Monuments to nature, whether animal, vegetable, or mineral in form, were mounted on walls or lined shelves—the Bella Abzug portrait a variation on the theme. All under a healthy layer of dust. He absently pulled the front curtain aside for a corner inspection. *Mold*.

"What are you *doing*, John?"

The curtain was dropped back into place, and he returned to the desk. Mrs. Gilroy spoke as she studied her screen. "So, you're from Silver Spring, Maryland. And what do you do for a living, Mister . . . Smith?" She gave him a sly wink.

John had no idea what that was for. Gert limped from display to display. "John is an engineer for the Environmental Protection Agency, Mrs. Gilroy."

"Ooh, that sounds like exciting work."

"I'm a bureaucrat. Surrounded by dullards."

"I'm afraid John's suffering through a mid-life crisis."

"Well, a week with us should transform your life, Mr. Smith!" She fixed an admiring gaze on the man who had given his life over to the highest calling, before moving forward with the registration process.

"Gender?"

"What?"

"Your *gender*, Mr. Smith?"

"Are you serious?"

Here John thought of his late, learned mother, who had taught him everything he would ever need to know about the speaking of proper English. Encompassing that "unique" did not come in degrees, and that "literally" meant *literally*. She had stressed, and made him repeat after her, that male and female were the *sexes;* and that gender applied only to language.

"In this enlightened age, Mr. Smith, we would never make light of anything so profound as gender."

"What do you think?"

"Mr. Smith, we would never presume. One's chosen place on the gender spectrum is an intensely personal decision."

"John has turned a deaf ear to the gender crisis, Mrs. Gilroy." Two woke women shared a glance. Oh. He was one of *those*.

Warned, now, as to the Augean task ahead, his hostess readied herself for a difficult road. But with the light that was about to shine on this austere man, the heart of the brave foresaw nothing short of redemption at the end of this, his odyssey. "Mr. Smith, the Borough of Progress officially recognizes eighty-one separate, and distinct, genders."

At that time of night—morning actually—John was in no mood for this woman's foolishness. "I guess I would be male. Is that on your list?"

"That would be 'Man.'"

"Put that."

Mrs. Gilroy made the notation.

"What about her?"

"I entered Mrs. Smith as 'Woman.'"

"Now you're getting the hang of it."

"Actually, you two are in luck. Our five-part Gender Studies Workshop begins every Monday, which just so happens to be . . . tomorrow!"

"Mrs. Gilroy, that is so exciting. I can't believe our good fortune."

"The course begins with An Introduction to Gender Science—One Gender, or Eighty-one? Why Choose? Followed on Tuesday by Pronoun Rundown: The Complete Guide."

"This one could stand some education. Sign us up."

"I will do that. Now, as to ethnicity . . ."

"What does our ethnicity have to do with anything?"

"John, stop being contrary."

"It's for the purpose of our Diversity Initiative, Mr. Smith. One step we can take to atone for our whiteness."

"Our skin color is some form of transgression? Who thought that up?"

"I've made it my life's work to make him aware of historical imbalances, Mrs. Gilroy."

Here it was again, his asserted white privilege thrown in his face. He couldn't recall a single instance where he had ever used color to his advantage. In fact, as far back as he could remember, promotions at EPA had *always* gone to women and minorities; job performance, even seniority, qualifications secondary to one's accredited victim standing. He worked now under some bossy foreign-sounding woman who didn't know back from forth.

"Why are we obliged to make amends for an accident of birth, Mrs. Gilroy?"

"You see what I mean, Mrs. Gilroy?" said Gert, putting her best foot forward for her new friend. "There's no concept of injustice."

"I thought you good people wanted to tear *down* the walls separating us," John ventured. "It seems to me like you're segregating us into ever-smaller groupings—that don't much like each other."

Who was this philistine? They didn't get many like him—and a good thing. "Inclusion is a worthy goal, Mr. Smith, but one needs travel different *avenues* . . . to reach one's destination."

"I hope we're not skewing your numbers." John's sarcasm lost on all but the speaker.

"Well, that is a concern."

It was getting along towards two. "How much longer is this going to take?"

"We're almost there, Mr. Smith."

Walking on rarefied air, Gert resumed her lobby stroll. John kept a wary eye on the keeper of the inn and mayor of Progress. How crazy was this bird? It was too soon to know precisely where this woman ranked on the lunatic scale. He hoped she wasn't dangerous.

Gert came to a framed action photo of a soccer game. "I love this shot, Mrs. Gilroy."

Mrs. Gilroy looked up, pleased. "Yes. That's the local *futbol* club."

"Are you kidding me?" John grumbled.

"There's a game every Friday. *Futbol* Night!"

Gert beamed. Mrs. Gilroy placed a form on the desk for John to fill out.

"John, look!"

Lo and behold, it was none other than Al Gore. A copy of the identical portrait adorned the corner nook above the fireplace. With a sorry shake of his head, John started on the form.

"I have a surprise for you tomorrow on your tour."

Gert was examining the various bric-a-brac. "Mrs. Gilroy, I think we're going to get along just fine."

"I'm certain that we will," she said, taking the form from John. "Now, is either of you HIV positive?"

An unequivocal male was thrown for a loop. "Why would you ask that?"

Her smile bespoke an altruism divine in essence. "There's a ten percent discount."

"This," said John, handing her his card, "is going to be a long week . . . And no, we're not."

She inserted the card, and slid it back, along with the receipt for his signature. "Now this amount contains the obligatory one hundred dollar donation to GALS."

"Dare I ask . . . ?"

"Why, it's the Gay And Lesbian Scholarship fund, of course."

"Of course. I think we'll pass on that one, Mrs. Gilroy."

"We'll be happy to contribute to the GALS, John."

"It's not *the* GALS, Mrs. Smith. It's just . . . GALS."

Why was he always the one to capitulate? One of these days. . . He sighed, and signed.

"Thank you very much, Mister (another wink) Smith."

Gert plopped down in a comfy chair. "Oh, John. This chair is wonderful. I just might spend the night right here."

"What was that for, Mrs. Gilroy?"

Their liberal hostess replied with another wink—and a knowing smile. "We understand . . . "

"Understand what?"

"Mr. *Smith*, your secrets are safe with us. In Progress we're possessed of the sweet song of a nonjudgmental spirit."

He finally got it. "You think I'm messing around? With *her*?"

Gert luxuriated in the chair. John couldn't stop laughing as he wrestled with the bags one last time.

# # #

The room was lifted from a log cabin. There were dressers, chairs, and tables of unfinished oak; the only amenities a rotary dial phone, a windup alarm clock at bedside, and an 18-inch TV set. Gert's heart filled. For stout progressives primitive accommodations epitomized sacrifice, by an elect among whom she most certainly was numbered. *Noblesse oblige.*

"This is wonderful. It takes one back to a simpler time."

As long as she has that damn phone, her husband thought. She rolled one of the carry-ons around to her side of the bed, while he handled the rest. Finished, he flopped onto threadbare bedding.

"Don't you dare fall asleep before you floss and brush, John."

She noticed a cardboard sign on the bureau. Took it in hand, smiling as she read. "Listen to this, John. 'Please do not swat the flies. They *too* want to enjoy their stay in Progress.'" She turned to him. "Isn't that cute?"

He was fast asleep. She noticed that there *were* a number of flies buzzing around. She opened the top drawer of the dresser and removed a copy of the *Koran*. "They've thought of everything."

As she moved about getting settled—waving at the flies—she noticed the little cutout boxes in each corner.

# # #

In darkness unbroken, the Smiths slept snuggled in the double bed. John awoke to the pitter-patter of tiny footsteps.

"Do you hear that?"

He sat up, and turned on the bedside lamp. Mice, by the dozen, ran to and fro, eating from the little boxes. He rousted his wife.

"Will you look at this?"

She sat up, silly from sleep, or the lack, rubbing her eyes. She went for the lamp—already on—and found her glasses. "Oh, dear."

A particularly engaging character perched on the night table, checking out the new residents. John swatted it away. "Are you kidding me?" He grabbed the phone, finger taking the long way around from zero. "I'm giving that nutty broad a call."

"She waited up for us, John. Let the poor woman rest."

Fanatics don't know from clocks. Mrs. Gilroy was still at work as the phone rang. "Good morning, Progress Inn." She listened. "Oh, good morning, Mister Smith! My goodness, you *are* an early riser."

"Mrs. Gilroy, there are mice running all over our room."

The good mayor was exultant. "Isn't it grand? Progress teems with wildlife."

The mice scampered about, happily munching from the little boxes, in what could be concluded was a nightly ritual.

"Mrs. Gilroy, I don't think this mouse poison is working."

He heard her laugh happily. "Oh, Mister Smith, you are a dickens, you are. That's not mouse poison . . . It's mouse *food*."

CHAPTER 6

Brittany

John was awakened by the jangling of the telephone. He fumbled for the receiver, inadvertently hanging it up. It rang again in seconds—guess who?—bright and cheery on the other end.

"Good morning, Mr. Smith. Did you sleep well?"

"I . . . was."

"I'm so glad to hear that," she began. "Mr. Smith, it's half-past eight. This is a friendly reminder that our Gender Studies Workshop begins in just thirty minutes."

"Your what?"

"Now, Mr. Smith. We spoke about it only last night."

John listened, quite patiently he thought, for a man whose sleep had been so rudely interrupted on the first day of his vacation.

"It's most popular, and, if I might add, an immensely enriching experience," she said, concluding a lengthy pitch.

John ran a hand over his tired face as she provided additional helpful information. "Six *hours*? Mrs. Gilroy, I think we'll pass on the workshop." He hung up.

It rang again. He yanked the receiver from its cradle. "Yeah."

"It's *encouraged*."

She heard the emphatic click.

# # #

They were arrayed in their best tourist outfits. His boisterous Hawaiian shirt draped like a tent over Bermuda shorts in an attempted cover-up. She, opting for a flowered blouse to go with black shorts, the better to accentuate squat legs of a lucent white. Warnings were directed his way regarding the pernicious effects of his golfer's tan; sun *damage* to the climate aware, who saw only the downside.

"Don't forget your sunblock, John. And just because you're wearing those flip-flops doesn't mean you can skip your foot powder." Not a morning person generally, she was especially testy that fine morning, having missed part one of the workshop. He had no right to make such a decision for them.

"I hate that shirt." She hoped he wasn't going to make an ass of himself the first day.

He was buttoning that shirt as he examined the lineup of bins, labeled respectively: Glass, Plastic, Paper, Non-recyclables, and a final bin marked only by a small image of Mother Earth. He opened the lid and screwed up his face.

"What is it?" she demanded, as she slathered sunblock from head to toe.

"There's stuff in here."

She capped the tube, and rose to enlighten.

"You look like Mount Kilimanjaro."

She was a respected environmental activist—and would be treated thus. Her pained reply to her adolescent husband was laced with condescension. "That's compost, John."

"It smells like dirt."

"Well, close the lid." The man was hopeless. "You work for the EPA, and you know nothing about compost. You really should get in touch with your world, John."

"Is that where we put the mouse droppings?"

"The maids will take care of that. Just watch your step, please."

# # #

"Good morning, Mrs. Gilroy," Gert chirped, as they entered the lobby.

A downcast Mrs. Gilroy was not receiving, or dispensing, pleasantries. "We missed you at the workshop."

"And I'm so sorry we missed it."

"You can still catch the afternoon session," she came back, spark rekindled.

Gert looked hopefully toward her husband, who nevertheless offered his kind regrets. "In that we've already fallen so far behind . . ."

"Oh, no, that should not be a problem," their hostess insisted.

"If it's all the same, Mrs. Gilroy, we think we'll just take the tour."

"But it's not all the same, John." Whatever that meant. She wasn't exactly sure, only that coming from him it didn't sound very sincere.

"Well, I guess we could do that," acknowledged the mayor, "but it would be highly irregular. The workshop always precedes the tour."

"Indulge us."

She turned to Gert. "We have a wonderful turnout, as always. Many of the local residents sit in on a regular basis. They find the seventy-five dollar donation a pittance for such uplift—and hope for a brighter tomorrow for our gender nuanced."

"Seventy-five dollars?" John coughed.

"Oh, but for guests of the inn it's complimentary. And encouraged."

On the wall near the desk hung a portrait of a man with long, unkempt hair and beard—and a look in his eyes to give Charles Manson pause.

"Who is that, Mrs. Gilroy?" Gert asked.

The query elicited a pronounced sigh. "That, I'm afraid, is the unfortunate *Mister* Gilroy."

# # #

The seven other tables in the adjoining cafe were empty. John and Gert studied their menus in silence; clear this reprobate husband would be taking his complimentary brunch in the doghouse.

"The woman was gracious enough to give you a second chance, John. The website says that workshop is one of the highlights of the Progress experience."

"I've come to terms with my ignorance."

There were times she could strangle him. He was going to ruin another vacation, and he made no bones about it. Well, she was going to that workshop tomorrow, with or without him. Look at him sitting there, hairless bulk in that ghastly shirt. He had already decided he was going to hate everything on the menu—she could see it in his eyes.

"There's two pepper shakers on the table, but no salt."

"Take one from another table," he was told.

He got up and checked several tables, returning empty-handed.

"They're trying to tell you something, John."

He had another look at the menu for The Deegan Vegan. It blared from every laminated page: *We love animals. We don't eat them.* He put the menu down. This promised to be seven days in hell. "I think I just lost my appetite."

She studied hers with a beatific smile. "It all looks so delicious, I don't know what to order."

John's back was to their approaching server. Before Gert had time to quietly implore him to please not stare, or worse, say something, she had reached the table. Gert cleared her throat in that cautionary vein her husband knew.

"Welcome to The Deegan Vegan. I'm Brittany." She was all perky Californian. You couldn't miss it.

There was reason to stare. Brittany was blond and curvy. But if there was a single dermal inch not involved in some tattoo, John couldn't find it. A safe assumption could be made for total coverage. He would have been more than happy to examine parts unseen, just to confirm. Brittany was really cute. Save for the tattoos, of course. And the piercings. For whatever blessed reason, the hair that could just as easily have been green or purple, was silky pure, long and full. To go with luminous blue eyes, and a sparkling smile. One thing you could say for Californians; they have great teeth. Maybe this vacation wouldn't be so bad after all.

Look at him, Gert thought. Passing judgment. The way he's looking her up and down. Don't stare, you dolt. Yes, the young woman has some tattoos. It's her form of *expression*.

Such exquisite construction beneath that "Good Cholesterol Sold Here!" T-shirt. John was thanking heaven for little girls.

"Good afternoon, Brittany," said Gert formally.

John went to hand her his menu. "Brittany, could we see the breakfast menu, please?"

Brittany giggled. "That is the breakfast menu. Would you like to start with something to drink?"

Gert ordered a glass of mountain spring water. "You *do* have mountain spring water?"

Brittany was writing on her pad. "The only kind we serve. It's amazing." She remembered, adding, "Paper straw okay? We're plastic straw free."

"Of course." Gert would have expected nothing less.

John rolled his eyes—and ordered coffee.

"Soy or rice creamer?"

"What?"

Gert looked up from her menu. "Go with the soy."

John said he would take the rice.

"Awwwe-some. Are you ready to order, or do you need more time?"

Fluent in vegan, and keen to flaunt it, Gert answered without consulting her partner. "I think we're ready. I'll have the gluten-free pancakes, with the organic apricot avocado salad."

John was feeling ill.

Brittany took it down, "Awwwe-some." She looked his way.

"I'll go with the bacon and eggs."

Brittany gushed with laughter. "Oh, Mr. Smith, you're so cute. Mrs. G warned me about you."

"I've been telling him for years we should go vegan," Gert replied with pharisaic finality. "Would you please get in the spirit, John?"

This was his life. Teachable moments, stretching from here to there. The old dog was hungry. "Is there a McDonald's in this town?"

Brittany laughed again, sweet and infectious. "Mr. Smith, I think you'd enjoy our Tofu Breakfast Scramble. It's amazing."

"Can I get scrapple with that?"

"They don't have vegan *scrapple*, John." Must he embarrass her this way?

"I don't even know what it *is*," said Brittany.

John had another question. "What exactly is tofu?"

"Oh good heavens." Gert wanted to crawl under the table.

"Tofu is made from soybeans, water, and a coagulant, or curdling agent," Brittany explained. "It's high in protein and calcium, and has been a staple of Asian cuisines for hundreds of years. It's much healthier than red meat."

John felt the noose tightening. His wife was in full accord.

"I've been trying to tell you, John, that red meat is behind your irritable bowel syndrome."

"I'm soooo over red meat," said Brittany, turning to John. "I used to have the same problem."

He glared across the table. Thanks.

"That was impressive, Brittany." Gert was feeling very much in her element.

Brittany smiled; humble. "I'm a student at the Vegan Culinary Institute in Corvallis. It's amazing. I intern here in the summer."

"Good for you."

"I want to save the Earth. And the Earth begins . . . with our bodies."

Did she have to go there? Already facing starvation, John grappling now with myriad male hungers.

"Brittany, I think the Earth is in capable hands," said Gert.

"Well . . ."

"How does the tongue piercing thing work?"

"John!"

Brittany laughed, not bothered in the least. "You get used to it."

"Tell us a little more about yourself, Brittany," said Gert, steering the conversation, she hoped, back in a positive direction.

"I'm from Cali-*farn*-ya. Van Nuys. It's in The Valley. I have three amazing sisters: Morgan, Mason, and Cody! They're awesome. They look up to me."

"I can see why."

"I started out at Berkeley, like my dad, but I'm so much happier at The Institute."

Gert smiled in admiration for this extraordinary young woman.

"Progress is *amazing*. Mrs. Gilroy is awesome."

Delirious from hunger, John was seeing visions. Brittany sashayed down a sun-drenched beach, the only thing whiter than the sand, her string bikini. She came to a stop and tossed her head back, running fingers through her golden hair as she scanned the horizon. Finally, she shed top and bottom—just casually flung them aside—and walked on. No one even noticed! Because the tattoos were a bodysuit. It was like that year in the swimsuit issue where the girls were totally naked, but it was okay because their bodies were painted.

"The tattoos. Are they any kind of protection in the sun?"

Brittany laughed happily.

"What kind of question is that, John? Just because she looks a little different."

"I get asked that a lot."

"You do?" The man could do no wrong with this girl.

"People tell me my body art is amazing."

Do girls with tattoos wear dresses? Feminists hate dresses because they're totally feminine, men like them, and they're not about to do anything to please men. John was picturing Brittany in one of those full-length dresses that were like a sack. The ones that really hugged the body. Maybe with an ankle bracelet. Yes. She would do just fine in one of those.

"Are you still with us, John?"

Roused from reverie, our oversexed sexagenarian had to think fast. "Tell me, Brittany, what would be the most amazing dish on the menu?"

"Hmm." Brittany pondered. "I'll have to cogitate on that."

"And we need a shaker of salt. There are none on any of the tables."

Brittany was suddenly struck uneasy. "Mr. Smith, I'm afraid we can't go there." She leaned in, voice barely above a whisper, blue eyes as wide as the sea.

"It's a $250 fine if you're even found to have salt on your person."

CHAPTER 7

Octavia

"You were flirting shamelessly."

"I was just being friendly."

They had entered the lobby from The Deegan Vegan.

"Humph. Pretending to actually enjoy tofu."

"I was getting into the spirit."

"That breakfast was awful, and you know it," she huffed. "And the way you were cozying up to that little freak. She was coming on to you, John."

They waited at the desk. "Is there a bell or something?"

"And since when are you the big tipper?"

"I felt sorry for her. We were probably the only customers she had all morning."

"California bimbo."

John reluctantly rang the bell, shoring up his defenses for day one in the land of the snowflakes. All he really wanted was to crawl back into bed.

His wife was still not finished with their server. "Progress is amazing... Mrs. Gilroy is *amazing*... My body is *a-MAY-zing!*"

# # #

The sun shone brightly as they stood on the top step for their first look down Main Street. In hiking boots and Tyrolean hat, Mrs. Gilroy was the picture of exuberance.

"What a glorious day!" She skipped down the steps into a joyous pirouette. "Welcome to Progress!"

In the harsh glare of that glorious morning, Main Street fell somewhere *short* of glorious. John and Gert took the steps one at a time as they gazed—dumbstruck.

Faded or unpainted buildings, and rutted dirt streets, rendered the look of an Old West town. Loose pieces of molding and siding hung next to fallen rain gutters. There were actual holes in walls. The roof of the building adjoining the inn was on the verge of collapse. Across the street, the front door of The Progressive bookstore was boarded up. Yes, We Are Open! read the spray-painted welcome. The Manic Organic advertised half off everything in their Going Out of Business Sale. Likewise, The Pet Shop Co-op; belly up.

A streetlamp hung by a wire from its pole. A "Speed Limit 20 km per hour" sign was posted—sideways. The traffic consisted entirely of bicycles, riders dutifully helmeted, maneuvering around the numerous puddles. John counted broken windows.

Gert was reeling—her hand to her heart—but John was still game. "Looks like this place could use a coat of paint."

"I should say . . ." slipped from Gert's lips.

Mrs. Gilroy was aghast. "Good heavens, Mr. Smith. And have chemicals fouling our air?"

"She's right, John," said Mrs. Smith, pivoting on a dime.

John shrugged. The horror exceeded even his expectations.

"I rather like a natural look," Gert managed to add, fooling no one.

Mrs. Gilroy proudly indicated the street sign. "As you can see, Progress is one hundred percent metric!"

John made a point of turning his head on its side to read it.

"Although I guess I should have José fix that." She smiled sympathetically. "José is dyslexic."

"That should be no barrier," said Gert with conviction.

"You are so right, Mrs. Smith. In fact, in the spirit of inclusion, all of the members of our public works department are physically challenged. We give a hand up . . . to those who might have difficulty gaining employment elsewhere. We think it's one of the areas that sets us apart."

"Isn't that wonderful. John, don't you think that's wonderful?"

That at least partly explained it. The place looked like a ghost town with people in it.

Their guide shielded her eyes from the sun as she looked down Main Street. "Here he comes now!"

Handsome, strapping José, 29, strode the sidewalk, nimbly sidestepping the cracks and crumbles. Mrs. Gilroy waved, all giggly and girlish, as he approached.

"Good afternoon, José."

José was the strong, silent type. Silent—as in speaking virtually no English. He politely acknowledged the Smiths.

"I hate to bring this up now, José," Mrs. Gilroy began, "with you having just met Mr. and Mrs. Smith. But isn't it time you got around to fixing that sign? It's been several years, I believe."

José just stared, uncomprehending.

She indicated the improperly hung sign. "The . . . sign?"

"*Signo. Si.*"

She smiled. They were making progress. "*Si, signo. Signo es,* uh, or, *esta . . .*" She groped for the word. "*Signo esta . . .*" She demonstrated a turning motion.

José turned to John and Gert with a shy smile. "*No hablo ingles.*" He peered at Mrs. Gilroy, trying hard to get a handle on the problem.

The mayor blundered on. "*Si . . . signo, uh, por favor . . .*" She tilted her head as if to read the sign. At last, José got the picture.

"*Si*, Mrs. Gilroy. *Si!*"

He nodded politely to John and Gert before hurrying off, on the job. Mrs. Gilroy and Gert fondly watched him walk away.

"He's a fine young man."

"He certainly is," Gert agreed.

"And an excellent worker."

John had held his peace throughout this clumsy exchange, not knowing whether to laugh, or pity this poor woman, tethered to an ideology that eschewed reason.

"I'm sure he is, Mrs. Gilroy, but . . . how the hell do you communicate?"

She was thinking aloud. "I must look up *sideways*."

"What about that streetlight?"

"Well," she admitted, "I'm afraid our dear José also suffers from a debilitating fear of heights."

They began a stroll down the mostly broken sidewalk. "Please watch your step. Progress has been as much a victim of budget constraints as any other municipality." Even as she spoke, a fissure caught her by the hiking boot—with John there to save her from falling.

"Oh, dear. Thank you, Mr. Smith." She paused to collect herself. Shook a resolute fist. "We must raise taxes."

That should do it, thought the visitor. He wondered how the lowly Progressive bookstore would fare under the increased tax burden.

Their escort clasped her hands. "Are we ready to begin our tour?"

"Oh, Mrs. Gilroy, I can't wait!"

"The first thing you may notice," she indicated as they resumed their walk, "is that our streets are unpaved. Progress's founding parents endeavored to build a community where man's intrusion into a wondrous and natural world was held to the barest of minimums."

Gert burst into excited applause. "Bravo, Mrs. Gilroy! Bravo!"

Interesting, John was thinking, how when speaking in condemnation, it was still acceptable to refer to humanity in the masculine.

"And with our bold interdiction of the internal combustion machine, Progressions can get high on the same pure air as that breathed by the *Native* Americans."

"Oh . . ." They had trodden this very earth. Felt it between their toes. For Gert, this went beyond the mundane, to the spiritual. And how to explain what she was *feeling*? Yes . . . she was on the verge of her first orgasm in eleven years.

The Orioles were in Detroit. The bats had come alive, but John had his doubts about the bullpen.

With Gert having regained her center, the tour resumed. As Mrs. Gilroy jabbered on—words escaping to the ether—John was struck by the number and tenor of the street signs: NO Littering!; NO Smoking!; Riders MUST Be Helmeted!; Hate Speech STRICTLY Prohibited!; Homeless *PLEASE* Curb Your Bodily Functions! For a loving and tolerant community, they did have their rules. Their jolly little mayor ruled with a velvet-gloved fist.

Coincident with what appeared from a distance to be a nude woman walking in their direction, John noticed one more: In the Interest of Freedom of Expression and Perception Transformationality—Dress, Or the Lack Thereof, is Strictly Optional. As the woman approached, John made out that she was not only comprehensively naked, but sumptuous of form, a golden-brown head to toe, wanton streaked hair bound in a bun.

"Keep your eyes to yourself, John."

"Why Octavia!" This was clearly someone Mrs. Gilroy admired.

"Good afternoon, Mrs. Gilroy." Octavia sounded tired. She carried a book, a towel, and a bottle of body oil.

"Serendipitous bumping into you, Octavia. It's the perfect opportunity for you to meet Mr. and Mrs. Smith. They're visiting us from Maryland."

"Oh. I have an aunt there. It's nice to meet you." She shook Gert's hand, and went for John's, before Gert slapped his away. "I'm on my way from the center, Mrs. Gilroy, heading for the beach. We finished a little early today," said she, very matter of fact.

The beach suddenly sounded like a *great* idea. Maybe later.

"Octavia leads the workshop! She left a lucrative career in the adult arts to blaze a new trail, and she hasn't looked back."

"Frankly, I got tired of being pawed by dirty old white men."

"Terrible," said John.

"Yes, it is," said Gert, rapier glare piercing her husband.

"Octavia is nationally recognized."

Come to think of it, John thought, she did look familiar.

"We're most fortunate that she has chosen Progress as base for her vital work."

Gert broached a delicate subject with trepidation. "So, this is how you . . . *dress* . . . for the workshop?"

"We like to let our hair down, Mrs. Smith," said Octavia with a tired sigh, as she brushed back stray locks. "It's just easier this way."

John could see that. In fact, what could a class or two hurt? He wasn't afraid to try new things. "What time do those workshops start?"

"Well knock me down, Mr. Smith. You've had a change of heart!"

"I guess I'll be seeing you two tomorrow, then," Octavia concluded. "We'll be needing a penis model, and, so far, there are only women and reassignees in the class. Mr. Smith, maybe you can help out." She smiled blandly, and headed for the beach.

John was beginning to like Progress; Mrs. Gilroy made new by her guest's willingness to explore new frontiers. But as they moved forward, that guest was informed—by a higher authority—that he would not be setting foot within a mile of that workshop.

They passed an abandoned storefront, home to a number of vagrants, before coming to a fetid alley, and the rear of a Chinese restaurant. A pair of raccoons had toppled garbage cans, rooting through them. Mrs. Gilroy was transported. "Oh, look! Aren't raccoons simply the dearest of critters?"

Mi Hong, the weathered little cook, burst out of the back door—Mandarin curses flying—swinging a weaponized broom at the little invaders.

"I guess that depends," John suggested, "on one's point of view."

Gert was terrified as the raccoons charged past, making their escape; Mi Hong at the sight of Mrs. Gilroy, and her look of outrage.

"I sorry, Mrs. Gilroy! I sorry."

"Mi Hong, how dare you strike a living thing! For *shame*."

"I sorry, Mrs. Gilroy." He called after the raccoons. "Hey, come back. Have some food."

Mrs. Gilroy shook her head with the solemnity befitting a heroic public servant. "That won't be necessary, Mi Hong."

Mi Hong hung his head.

"You know, Mi Hong, we've had reports about you."

Mi Hong looked as sorry as a man can.

"Tales of diners finding dead animal flesh in some of your dishes."

"Not true, Mrs. Gilroy. No dead animal fresh. No dead animal fresh, *ever*."

"I'll take you at your word, Mi Hong. As for the raccoons, you know that in Progress every living thing is sacrosanct."

Mi Hong didn't know those big American words liberal white ladies liked to use, but he got the gist. He nodded vigorously—arms wide in avowal of his unfailing commitment to inclusion—be it man, or tree-dweller. "Evvy-body welcome."

What calamity of fate had delivered this unfortunate little man to this benighted dot on the globe? An expatriate, no doubt looking back on a youth, sunny by comparison, lived in service to Chairman Mao.

He bowed to Mrs. Gilroy and the Smiths, before seeking asylum in his kitchen. Mrs. Gilroy turned to John and Gert with a self-satisfied smile. "As you can readily see, being mayor is a full-time job."

Gert shrieked, and jumped into John's arms, as a rat raced past. She was sobbing into his shoulder—shaking uncontrollably—as the little varmint made a right turn, and scooted off in the direction of the inn.

"Are you alright, Mrs. Smith?" their guide asked kindly.

"Mrs. Gilroy, that thing scared me half to death!"

"I'm sure he meant you no harm."

Bewildered—putting it mildly—John gazed at the curious stranger while comforting his wife. "Does Progress have a rat problem, Mrs. Gilroy?"

The mayor seemed unnerved by the question, but for a politician her answer was a revelation in its candor. "We've never looked at it that way, Mr. Smith. We have rats . . . but we don't consider them a *problem*."

Gert freed herself from her husband's hold, her laugh self-conscious, bordering on embarrassed. "All this wildlife. I guess I'm just a city girl."

"It was a *rat*, Gert."

Here, John hit pause. Had they, in the course of their journey, passed through a portal, a wormhole maybe, gateway to some bizarro unreality? Where six thousand years of civilization had been turned on its head? Where up, was down—and down was *sideways*? That was the only plausible explanation.

Two sojourners in a Shangri-La fallen on hard times dumbly followed the woman in the boots and funny hat. A dark, imposing Gothic structure loomed, the most ornate building in Progress.

"The Second Progress United Earth Church of Universal Love and Tolerance. Mrs. Smith, perhaps a visit inside would provide you with some solace."

"The second. What happened to the first?" John inquired, with mischief aforethought.

He had found a sore spot. Behind steely eyes, images were wrought of conflict. Storm-tossed seas crashed. Ill winds blew. And the shore... littered with the *human* wreckage.

"We don't talk about it."

The concrete steps listed severely. John made his way to the top, and read aloud from the brass plaque:

"In a oneness void of stain,
and the stillness of time,
arms of every color embrace organic truth.
A thousand tongues merge into a universal language
of love;
hope;
trust;
and nonjudgmental understanding and acceptance,
of all, and for all.
Hands lift to our Mother Gaia;
to your seas of blue,
hills of green,
and rivers of white.
Our eyes to Father Uranus;
home of sun,

> and sender of life-giving rains.
> To Heaven and Earth we bow,
> in humble reverence,
> and perfect peace.
> Imperishable.
> Secure in our eternal home,
> the foreverness of The Cosmos."

Gert was welling up.

"Are you alright, Mrs. Smith?"

Amid a welter of sentiments, the visitor dabbed her eyes. "I've never heard such thoughts—my thoughts—expressed so beautifully."

John had fist to sternum. "Gets you right here."

"My cup runneth over."

Mrs. Gilroy was touched deeply. "What wonderful words, Mrs. Smith."

"Thank you, Mrs. Gilroy," Mrs. Smith sniffed.

"For what, my child?"

Gert looked about her. "For all of this."

"To simply be washed in your joy . . ."

The two women fell into each other's arms. The foregoing rivers flowed.

"Good afternoon, Mrs. Gilroy." Officer Shondra McCoy, 25, had ridden up on her bicycle. At a shade under five feet, a wee martinet in blue. Bonding event over, two middle-aged white females separated, wiping away tears.

"I hope I'm not interrupting anything."

"Good day, Officer McCoy! Certainly not. We were simply swept up in the wonder of being women in this beautiful place. Please join us." Whereupon the three embraced, blubbering like babies—John the graceless outsider at a quintessentially female moment. With his dispassionate powers of observation, he noted that Officer McCoy carried not a weapon, unless one were to so consider the whistle hanging from her neck.

Mrs. Gilroy laughed when they finally separated. "I guess we got a little carried away there." The others concurred, tittering and snuffling and blowing, while John waited patiently.

"Mr. and Mrs. Smith, Officer McCoy is a proud member of our all-female justice force. Another municipal feature that sets Progress apart."

Officer McCoy attempted a high five that missed, followed by a fist bump that connected, leaving the mayor rubbing bruised knuckles. "Whoo! Sisterhood!"

"Banishing the patriarchy, that bastion of white male supremacy in law enforcement, to the dustbin of history!" *A chorus of angels sang!*

"What the *hell*?" John asked aloud, looking all around him. Searching doors and windows and rooftops, eyes darting from this side of the street, to that. Where the *hell* . . . ?

The women had gone about their business, with Mrs. Gilroy yammering about their ridiculous police department, and Officer McCoy pumping her little fist in support. There had to be some explanation. *The Twilight Zone* was only a TV show, John reminded himself. Get a grip, man. He was not going to let these women—or this place—get to him. Could it have been his imagination? Was the dementia infectious? No. A thousand times, no. He *knew* what he had heard.

"What a triumphant idea!" Gert exclaimed; celestial choirs presumably commonplace within the corridors of the woke.

"And in declaring an end to the twin scourges of racism and sexism, an end to the brutality, and an end to mass incarceration, the good women of Progress resolved to stand tall." Officer McCoy evidently excepted.

To witness, to be part of an unfolding miracle, Gert was uplifted as never before; John left nosing around for wind of angels.

"Anything they can do, we can do. Whoo!" exulted Officer McCoy, all 97 pounds—to include uniform—leaping to give Mrs. Gilroy another five.

"Whoo!" whooped the mayor.

Trying hard not to laugh, John had a question. "How do you maintain order?"

"Excuse me, Mr. Smith?"

"Sometimes people do bad things."

"I'm not sure I follow."

"I don't see a gun on Officer McCoy."

The good mayor blanched. Dazed, by a blow she hadn't seen coming. She fought for control, of her emotions, of her will to carry on in the face of reckless words that spoke only of hate. Fear and trembling seized her as she clutched her ample bosom. "Good heavens, Mr. Smith. There is no place for firearms in Progress."

John shrugged, eminently reasonable. "What about a Taser? A Taser never hurt anybody."

"Oh-dear-me." She was fanning feverishly.

He was having fun. "Mace? . . . Nightstick? . . . Anything?"

Officer McCoy dug in her little heels, but Her Honor was failing. "Mr. Smith, Mr. Smith. Goodness, goodness," she said, mopping drops of blood from her brow. The mere *thought* of physical force made her quake. She was dry sobbing pitifully as she clung to Officer McCoy.

"Are you alright, dear?" Gert asked, solicitous hand reaching out. And to go with that look of revulsion reserved exclusively for wayward husbands—"Look what you've done to Mrs. Gilroy!"

But this *prophetess*—immaculate in word and deed—was nothing if not resilient. "I'll be alright, Mrs. Smith." A tsunami of peace and justice was set to be loosed on the world, and she would be there to usher in the new day. Possessed of the nobility of the straight, she issued in proclamation: "The women of Progress stand united."

"United. Really? What about diverse?"

All-knowing though she may be, did this interloper have to keep asking such hard questions? "Well . . . that too."

"Mrs. Gilroy and her values are not on trial, John."

It would go down in the annals. The people's stalwart stared down her foe—and the ignorance he personified. Her delivery was even, its tone vastly superior. "This is a peace-loving community, sir. We've evolved to a better place."

"Wait till word gets out."

"Ever the cynic, John."

"Keep up the good work, Officer McCoy," the mayor sniffed.

Officer McCoy saluted before riding off.

Smiling sardonically, it was more quip than question. "If I might beg your pardon, Your Honor. What exactly does she do besides hand out parking tickets?"

"I apologize for my husband's patronizing attitude, Mrs. Gilroy."

"All I can say is, I hope we're outta here before all hell breaks loose."

Across the street, the Gender Studies Center was a gleaming three-story structure of red brick and shiny aluminum. A sight to stoke progressive fires. Their astral overseer put on a magnanimous smile—set to forgive. Head high, she announced: "We'll be breaking ground on the new wing of the Gender Studies Center in the coming spring."

"The new *wing*?" John chuckled at the thought.

"Why, yes. It will house the laboratory expansion."

The events of that first evening and afternoon had comprised the most intense of endurance tests for a rational mind like John's. A week's worth of nonsense crowded into the first twelve hours. "Forgive my lack of awareness . . . but . . . what exactly do they study?"

It was a pity.

"What can I possibly say, Mrs. Gilroy?"

"I'm afraid he said it, Mrs. Smith."

"I don't know whether to laugh, or cry."

"Never fear, dear one. I see hope for him yet."

When logic, hard evidence, or real science expose their settled truths to cold-eyed analysis, the vainglorious Left need only turn to that greatest of all nullifiers: pious condescension.

"Mr. Smith, it is for Octavia and her groundbreaking team to explore the mysteries . . . and dispel the *myths* . . . of gender."

"Can you give us an example?" laughed John from the winning side. "Mystery or myth? Take your pick."

"Oh, stop it, John. You're making a fool of yourself."

Their all-seeing arbiter of good and evil was undaunted. "All of your questions should be answered, and more, Mr. Smith, now that you'll be participating in the workshop."

"I'll take notes."

Her husband was beginning to bore her. Gert was ready to move forward, her focus down the street.

"Is that what I think it is, Mrs. Gilroy?"

CHAPTER 8

The Chief

John found the number of shuttered storefronts and boarded-up buildings troubling, but Mrs. Gilroy seemed not to notice. When he artlessly called them to her attention, the mayor was unfailingly upbeat in the knowledge that with virtue on their side, a splendid recovery was surely just around the corner.

They came to the object of Gert's fascination, what otherwise looked like a chain of vacant lots, filled with pile after pile of an obscure substance.

"The crown jewel of our civic pride," declaimed the mayor, "The Mildred McFadden Pavilion at The Progress Compost Repository."

There was a mouthful. The pavilion was a mostly glass structure, its entrance a pagoda-like enclosure. Gert's eyes were wide with wonder.

"Mrs. Gilroy, it's magnificent!"

"Let's go inside!"

Admission was only $15 a head. There were literature displays, a Q&A center, and a stand dispensing free organic lemonade to wash down the granola bars—a bargain at five dollars apiece. On a large screen played a twenty-minute loop on the joys of composting, and the divers ways it served the planet. John couldn't recall when he had last seen that many people, having that much fun.

Their guide was effluent with little-known facts and anecdotes. "At our computer center you can take a thirty-minute virtual tour, down through the *history* of The Repository."

"Mrs. Gilroy, how exciting!" Gert was soaring.

"It's one of our most popular attractions."

Her protegee selected brochures from several of the displays.

"And beginning next month, you will be able to take the tour online. Fun for the whole family."

Gert was leafing through the brochures. "We'll be starting our pile the moment we get home, Mrs. Gilroy." She spotted a life-sized cutout of the late Mildred McFadden, patroness of the movement. The little woman with the heart of a lion—*radiant!*—a humble servant dwarfed by the mountain of compost at her side.

"This must be Ms. McFadden."

"One of the most beloved figures in our state's history." Their guide broke off, overcome. "I'm sorry," she uttered breathlessly. "This should not be this difficult."

John thumbed through a paperback on the Lewis and Clark expedition, conjuring visions: the accumulated compost left behind each time the company broke camp. He hoped the Native Oregonians had put it to good use.

Gert consoled her sister and inspiration; her fate, to abide a decadent and squalid world. "You take all the time you need, dear."

She patted Gert on the hand. After a deep breath, and drawing from her the fiber of endurance, prepared to forge ahead. "Mildred McFadden was our Gandhi. It was she who, looking down the barrel of apathy, brought composting to the Borough of Progress."

Misty eyes met, and floodgates opened. Joy, mingled with the pain of loss. At the end, it was Mrs. Gilroy a support for her new friend. Gert wanted to put her Kleenex away, but the tears kept coming.

"Mrs. Gilroy, you don't understand. My friend Leslie and I will be all alone in this. There just isn't the will back home. It's a dark place."

"*Au contraire, ma soeur, au contraire.* There are support groups in every state. You need only find the one in your community. Our website has the listings!"

"Oh, Mrs. Gilroy. You are so *good.*"

John would have thought the wells to have run dry by that point, but they were at it again. He replaced his book on the shelf and headed for the exit.

Outside the glass walls, a resistance had formed: a dozen or so women, and a lone bearded male. What was his story? With the difficulty distinguishing between varying shrill expostulations, John couldn't tell exactly *what* had them so agitated. Their problem was either with men—or carbon. He thought he had caught something about emissions mixed in there. The single picket sign toted by the subservient white male—an expedient in the event of this, or other required heavy lifting—carried the catch-all Resist Hate! message. A spontaneous uprising, no doubt, directed at unfeeling humanity in general; with him, the bald-headed middle-aged white male, a likely bald-faced offender. Several—the less attractive, unfortunately— had removed their clothing to more effectively drive their point home; whatever it was.

In an act of naked aggression, an unidentified projectile was fired in his direction. Fortunately for John, it missed by a wide margin. Something had been balled up in rubber bands. He disarmed what he determined to be a bra—and put the evidence in his pocket.

"Me too, could it be you?"

"Me too, could it be you?"

"Me too, it could be you!"

Were they accusing *him* of something? To his knowledge he had never forced himself on anyone; not in the last four decades anyway. But, then, the college years were a bit of a blur.

Bearing the pacific smiles of the anointed, his wife and the mayor emerged from the little pagoda. The mayor carried a copy of *Progressive Composting* magazine, which she promptly presented to John.

"Mrs. Gilroy, you're too kind."

"Read it at your leisure, Mr. Smith. I'm sure you'll find it most informative."

"He's not going to read it, Mrs. Gilroy."

John looked out on pile upon pile dotting the landscape. "They couldn't put a fence around it or something?"

"It's nature, John."

"What do they do with it?"

A perfectly reasonable question was too much for the erudite, the paroxysm of laughter touched off bringing the women almost to their knees.

"Oh, John."

"Mrs. Smith, we've a long way to go, I'm afraid."

The mayor continued to tout their environmental bona fides. "We're a *six-time* recipient of the Governor's Certificate of Merit, and, one of the finalists for Composting Community of the Year."

"Oh, Mrs. Gilroy, you must be so excited."

"Oh, we are. We're trying not to get our hopes up, but," she added confidentially, "I have a friend in the governor's office, and she tells me that this may be our year." She held up both hands, fingers tightly crossed.

"What a boon for tourism."

"John, how dare you rain on Mrs. Gilroy's parade."

She had suffered enough of his churlishness for one afternoon, but the mayor dismissed the little gibe with a self-assured smile. "Not to worry, Mrs. Smith. We hear the naysayers, and it just goes in one ear, and out the other."

"Not gonna *touch* that one."

"Oh, stop your mumbling."

They resumed their stroll past baleful glares, the resistance yielding to the woke mayor. An old abandoned factory was now the Progress Recycling Center, a large, bustling facility.

"And in answer to all those critics who say we're not business-friendly, we present our state-of-the-art recycling center."

The quasi-private center appeared to be the *only* prosperous enterprise in Progress.

"The largest and most technologically advanced recycling center west of the Mississippi! We have guided tours at ten and two, and a Spanish tour at three-thirty."

Gert looked at her watch, and back at John. He busied himself in introspection, before taking her quietly aside. "How should I put this?" After a sidelong glance, he placed one hand firmly on each shoulder, and looked his wife squarely in the eye. "We came three . . . thousand miles . . . for *this*?"

The woman who had given the best forty-two years of her life to this man was incredulous. Well she knew his lack of patience, but could he be *this* obtuse? "The tour is just getting started, John," she stated expressly, leering at her ponderous partner as she rejoined their guide.

His every move watched, he drifted to the curb, steeped in regret. She'd done it again. He pulled a cigar out of his shirt pocket and opened it, blithely leaving cellophane to flutter to undefiled dirt street. He lit it, and puffed with satisfaction, savoring that rarest of moments—one of pure pleasure.

A whistle sounded. Onlookers gasped. Officer McCoy was Johnny-on-the-spot, ticket book drawn.

"John!"

Officer McCoy held out her little hand. "ID."

John shrugged, took out his wallet, and handed her his driver's license. "Smoking is a serious offense in the Borough of Progress, Mr. Smith," she said in peremptory fashion, handing him the ticket.

"Two hundred dollars?"

"You should have known better, John."

"We strive to set an example for our *children*, Mr. Smith," said the mayor with feeling.

Officer McCoy wasn't finished. "And this is for littering."

John had a look at the second ticket. "*Three* hundred dollars?" He appealed to Madam Mayor. "Can't I just pick it up?"

Officer McCoy handed his license back. "Thank you—and have a pleasant day."

"Great job, Officer McCoy! Keep up the good work."

She saluted her superior and rode off.

# # #

The town square was an aesthetic respite from progressivist squalor. Benches and verdant landscaping surrounded a prominent statue that looked down on a dry fountain. Arms unfurled, Mrs. Gilroy made her presentation.

"Our Town Square."

"How lovely, Mrs. Gilroy."

She looked John's way, awaiting affirmation. It certainly was a welcome sight. He could see himself there, whiling away the hours with a good book. But the devil in him couldn't resist. "Where's the water?"

Mrs. Gilroy put on her politician's hat. "Well, with passage of our new H2-Zero conservation measure, we're not able to actually run the fountain."

"What a shame," Gert uttered, before catching herself. "But we must not squander the Earth's resources."

Mrs. Gilroy directed their attention to the statue. Gert's eyes lit up like a schoolgirl's. A twelve-foot bronze image of His Eminence towered over them. In one hand he held the Earth, in the other a tree.

"Oh, shit."

"Oh, Mrs. Gilroy!"

"Your eyes deceive you not," confirmed the mayor, on the threshold of nirvana.

"He's got the whole world in his hands."

"In one hand," said the husband, in the interest of accuracy.

"Mrs. Gilroy, this makes the entire trip worthwhile."

"Vice President Al Gore Park!"

John turned to walk away.

"You don't approve, Mr. Smith?

"The vice president's an eco-hustler, according to my John."

"Mr. Smith doesn't genuflect for climate billionaires."

Patent blasphemy. But his wife's liberal breast swelled in the knowledge that this pagan was powerless to profane sacred ground. She lifted her gaze, eyes luminous. "He lights my path."

But, even as one woman exulted, the other mourned the death of a dream. "He'll always be *our* president," she warbled.

The two women fell into each other's arms once more, weeping uncontrollably, forever captive to the delusion. That there had been any difference, beyond the cosmetic, between two insufferable dunces.

John waited it out. Bouquets of dead flowers blanketed the feet of the idol. He wondered to which island paradise the puffed-up god of Prius

Nation had flown that week to collect his quarter mil, underwritten by worthy interests at taxpayer expense. Followed by a little R&R in the tropical sun. Let the critics point fingers; the sycophants knew his *heart* to be pure.

Mrs. Gilroy produced a pair of fresh handkerchiefs, and the women mopped up. It had been an emotional afternoon.

"The monument was dedicated last April during our annual Earth Day Festival. The most joyous day of the year!" Set to burst, she at last made her revelation. "The vice president *himself* was here for the occasion."

"Mrs. *Gilroy*." The thought was dizzying. Fit to swoon, head swimming, she was ecstatic; clutching at her husband. She saw him astride his white steed, coming on the clouds. Let go—she was steadier now—elevated by signs and ethereal visions. "Oh, if only . . ." She dropped to her knees, arms outreached. "I feel his aura."

"Get it together, Gert."

"He called Progress the model for what America *could* be," said their spirit guide.

John chewed on that little tidbit.

"Could I have a moment, Mrs. Gilroy?"

"Certainly, my child," she said, whisking John away, whispering in his ear as they exited the square. "She needs time."

The resistance closed in as they crossed the street to Justice Force headquarters. "A splendid day it was. His motorcade encircled the square!"

"His motorcade. What about the ban?"

"The ban? Oh. Well. The vice president!"

# # #

All was quiet inside with the exception of one window, and a line of at least a dozen people. John was curious. "What's that line for, Mrs. Gilroy?"

"That's the cashier."

Gert rejoined them, wiping red eyes. Behind the counter posed an Olympian figure of tertiary gender; if they could even be so classified, gender a bare construct in Progress and environs. Somewhere in the official record existed a name, but she was known simply as The Chief. Preferred pronoun—The Chief was a traditionalist at heart—still an old-school "she." Subject to the caprices of wokeness. The Chief's anatomical configuration, current or congenital, nobody's damn business. Her dark uniform couldn't hide muscles out to here, but no uniform cap had ever been known to muss the spikes of blond and purple. Heavy makeup (John wondered if the stuff came off); fierce tattoos (*they* didn't); piercings (now *that* must have hurt); and accessory chains (no weak links on *this* mamma) graphically set The Chief apart as formidable adversary, and social justice crusader for the new millennium.

"Good afternoon, Chief!" The Chief was a particular favorite of the mayor's. She turned to address John and Gert. "I'd like for you to meet The Chief of the Progress Justice Force. And Chief, these are the Smiths. They're visiting us from Maryland."

The Chief wasted no time getting down to business, challenging John in her husky baritone. "Here to pay your fines?"

In Progress, money spoke the language. "Actually, I thought I'd ponder my missteps for a day or two, Chief."

"Looks like we've got a smartass on our hands, Mrs. Gilroy."

"Mr. Smith just has his own unique brand of humor, Chief."

"We're gonna be keeping an eye on you, buster."

"I appreciate that, Chief."

The mayor put on a happy face. "So, how is Sam?"

The thaw was palpable. John even thought he detected a trace of natural blush under the fake stuff.

"Sam's fine. Should be here any minute."

"Sam and The Chief are getting married on Saturday. I'll be giving The Chief away!"

John turned to Gert. "I guess you never know."

"I heard that," barked The Chief. "What the hell's that supposed to mean?"

"Just that one would think you'd be quite the catch, Chief."

"You know, this guy's asking for a fat lip, Mrs. Gilroy."

"Show some respect, John."

Mrs. Gilroy patted The Chief on the hand. "You just think happy thoughts, Chief, and look forward to your big day." She turned to Gert. "Sam and The Chief make such a handsome couple. It's going to be the social event of the season!"

John couldn't wait to meet her intended. Maybe the guy with the beard.

"I only wish we could be there for you, Chief."

"The whole town's invited, Mrs. Smith. You're welcome to come . . . as long as you don't bring this cretin."

Mrs. Gilroy lit up. "Here's Sam now!"

Black leather-wrapped head to toe, she had stepped from the pages of *Vogue*. African American, tall and slinky, her beauty suffused the room. Emerald eyes shone from beneath a mountain of relaxed hair, her white smile reaching from cheekbone to cheekbone. The low-slung red top show-cased a rich brown cleavage John adjudged to be real; incongruous to this girl pencil, but it made him gulp. Jewel-studded pants caressed legs longer than Gert, perched atop stiletto heels.

"Hello, Mrs. Gilroy," purred a sultry feline.

"It's wonderful to see you, Sam!"

It was a rare occasion indeed when John was speechless. And not a little green; a phantasmic rush, strictly male in color, madly crossing synapses. He felt the need to pinch himself. Where did they *find* these women?

Sam strode around the counter. The Chief took her in her arms and they shared a peck, love in their eyes.

"Where you been, babe?"

She held up her hand for The Chief to examine. "I broke a nail and had to get it fixed."

"Poor baby."

"I knowww..." she pouted.

How? *Why?* Gert was audaciously silent. Was this too much—even for her?

Mrs. Gilroy saw it too. "The Chief and Sam met last year on our singles cruise."

The Chief looked into Sam's eyes. "It was love at first sight."

They held their hands together, eyes never straying from the other's. "My parents objected at first."

"How narrow-minded," John interposed.

The Chief still felt the pain. "Just because I'm white."

Sam smiled tenderly, and gave her a reassuring nudge. "But now they're eager to welcome Chief to the family."

"All's well that ends well." John loved happy endings.

Gert was doing her best. This was diversity at its zenith. The fruit borne of the struggle. An intersectional mishmash that reimagined *everything*. "Will you be married in the church?"

"Of course." Sam gazed starry-eyed at The Chief. "I've always wanted a church wedding."

"Well," said John, "looks like you found the right church for it."

Sam reluctantly separated from her bride?/groom? to be. "I have to run. Will you be home early?"

"Not tonight, babe. I gotta go to the gym."

"Monday. I forgot." An awestruck little girl turned to Gert. "She's so *strong*."

She smiled sweetly before gliding out, blowing The Chief a kiss as she passed through the door.

Mrs. Gilroy appealed to the woman in Gert. "Don't you just love a wedding!"

The bank alarm sounded.

The Chief leapt over the counter, and charged out the front door.

CHAPTER 9

They were just in time to witness the battered pickup truck splashing through the puddles, the alleged perpetrator in the latest holdup at Progress Federal laughing and drumming on the wheel. Officer McCoy followed—peddling furiously—blasting away on her whistle.

For The Chief, this was personal. A slap at her department. "That son-of-a-bitch." She bolted back inside. "On it, Mrs. G!"

Mrs. G scurried down the street, picking up the chase.

John could only laugh. "Where does she think she's going?"

There was nothing to do but follow. They caught up with the overwrought mayor just past the church.

"Looks like word's out."

"I hope you're happy, John."

"This is the third time in a month he's robbed our little bank."

"The same guy?"

She nodded ruefully.

"Thank goodness for the FDIC."

"It's terrible," said Gert.

"And what about that internal combustion machine?" John was patently offended. "Who does this guy think he is?"

They continued gaping down the street, as if that might somehow bring back robber and loot. Amid this fury of inaction, the pickup, in fact, did—with a cheery squeak from its brakes—pull to a stop from behind. The pistol-packing suspect got out, cigarette clenched in his teeth.

"Extinguish that cigarette immediately, sir!" commanded the mayor.

The alleged perpetrator walked up to John. His Dodger cap was worn backwards. He was tall and lean, and except for the wraparound goatee—like Robert DeNiro in *Heat*—didn't look like a bank robber. "Gimme your wallet."

Gert was outraged. "How dare you!"

He pointed the gun at her.

"Give him your wallet, John."

"And gimme yours too, lady."

Gert reached in her purse and handed him her wallet forthwith. Opening it, he examined her driver's license. "Maryland, huh." He shook his head with a wry smile. "All you people, comin' all this way." He gave it another look. "That's a nice picture of you, lady. Real pretty."

"Why, thank you." She smiled, fixing her hair. "I haven't heard that from him in years."

"Well?" he said to John.

"She always looks the same."

"Your *wallet*, smart guy."

"Not until you put out that cigarette."

"What?"—gun back on John.

John handed it over. "Relax, fella."

He went through the wallets, pulling a clutch of fifties from John's—

"There goes that four hundred."

—before handing them back.

"You can keep the plastic, folks. This is cash and carry," he announced with a customer-friendly smile.

Gert put hers back in her purse. "That was nice of him," she said in an aside.

The piercing whistle announced their arrival. Having relentlessly tailed her suspect around the block, Officer McCoy and bike skidded to a stop behind the pickup. "Drop that gun!" she ordered, dismounting. "You're under arrest."

"Is that so," replied the suspect. "Funny, I don't *feel* under arrest."

With the mayor watching helplessly, the arresting officer had the weapon turned on her.

"You'll never get away with this," she told him, putting her hands up.

"I've gotten away with it three times so far, little lady."

As the alleged perpetrator stuffed the Smiths' cash in his pocket, Officer McCoy sprang into action with a sublethal kick to the shins.

"Officer McCoy!" Mrs. Gilroy cried in alarm.

"Ow. That hurt." The suspect sidestepped a second little boot, before pointing the gun back at his assailant. "You pissin' me off, little sista."

"This is a peace-loving community, sir," spoke the mayor—less than empowered.

"She kicked *me*."

"He's right, Officer McCoy. Violence is never the answer."

She came at him again, arms flailing with fists and karate chops, succeeding only in knocking his hat to the sidewalk. She was all huff and puff, down in her crouch, ready for more.

The alleged perpetrator picked up his hat and dusted it off. "You don't be messin' with my hat."

"Where, may I ask, is The Chief?" John inquired of the mayor, returning his lifeless wallet to his pocket.

"Manning the command post," Officer McCoy shot back from her stance. The chatter on her mobile radio concerned the detention of another smoker, four blocks away.

"So where's your backup?" John asked.

"Coming for you, you bastard," she readily informed her apprehended, under the potentially fatal delusion she held him at bay. Her quarry wore an easy smile. The coast was clear. One look at Madam Mayor's pitiable expression, and John knew Officer McCoy was on her own.

This member of Progress's finest *knew* she could do anything a man could—she had seen it in the movies—but her suspect rudely refused to get with the program. He dodged another wild swing, and in a toxic masculine exhibit took her under one arm—writhing and kicking—and carried her across the street, where she was deposited, unceremoniously it should be noted, in a ready pile of compost. He sauntered back, picked up her bike, and with his bare hands broke off the front wheel.

"That little girl should get defunded."

"Would you like to talk, sir?" Mrs. Gilroy asked.

"Talk about what?"

"Poor choices."

The mayor's sorry attempt at conflict management made the suspect smile. "You be trippin', lady." He looked over at John—"Is she for real?"—before calmly making his way to the door of the pickup. "Y'all have a peaceful day, now."

They watched impotently as he drove off. Officer McCoy made her meek return, brushing leaves and seeds from her uniform. She picked up bicycle in one hand, wheel in the other—"Chief's not gonna like this"—and trudged off.

She still enjoyed the mayor's full support. "Solid work, Officer McCoy!"

"This," said John, "is gonna make a *hell* of a report."

Mrs. Gilroy stood wringing her hands.

It seemed to John that the situation called for some form of action. "Aren't you going to do anything?"

"What *can* we do?"

"You could start with a call to the state police."

"What if he has a family?"

"He just robbed your *bank*." Here, John exercising maximum powers of restraint.

"I think first of a person's humanity, Mr. Smith. And besides," acknowledged the mayor, weighing legal ramifications, "we could face issues with profiling. We didn't actually *see* him rob the bank."

"She's right, John."

"A person of interest . . . regardless of the color of their skin . . . is innocent until proven guilty," added the mayor virtuously.

"Who said anything about skin color?"

"Your bias is *implicit*, Mr. Smith," she reflected sadly.

"What about equity, John?"

Was it the estrogen? George Soros? Was 5G already claiming brain cells? Like the proverbial blind man in a dark room, groping for a black hat that isn't there—or one living in California—John felt reality slipping from his grasp.

"You watched him rob *us*."

"Mr. Smith," the trusted public servant intoned from the saddle of her anti-racist high horse, "it is not ours to judge. He may come from a disadvantaged background."

\# \# \#

"I'm already out nine hundred dollars."

"You have only yourself to blame."

"That woman is touched."

She was busy sweeping while he relaxed on the bed, channel surfing on the little black and white TV. *Progressive Composting* rested on the night table.

"That woman is a visionary."

He waved at a fly. "Gert, this place is chaos."

"Every community has its challenges, John." She swept the accumulated mouse debris into a dustpan, and straightened up. "Although I'm surprised a four-star resort would have you clean your own room."

"We're all members of the human family, like your visionary friend said. Remember?" His annoyance was mounting. "Where the hell is the Golf Channel?"

He jumped a few more. Gert dumped her pan, and began folding his clothes. "I don't know why I should be doing this."

"There's no baseball. All they have is the damn soccer channel."

"Why don't you watch that?"

"You might as well ask me to watch women's basketball."

From an index finger dangled John's evidential bra. "What . . . is *this*?"

In what from appearances looked like a sticky situation mitigated by his complete innocence, John knew he stood on solid legal ground. But exoneration could be an exhaustive process where it concerned wives—comprising airtight alibis, incontrovertible evidence, the testimony of two witnesses, and more. Under normal circumstances leaving alien bras to be discovered in pants pockets was bad form for any husband, but in John's case the truth would set him free.

"I was the victim of an assault."

He should have known better. White men were not victims. White men were predators. "You probably stole it from one of those poor activists," she said, throwing some other woman's refuse next to him on the bed. "If that's how you get your kicks, you and Jennifer can have your fun," she snarled, alluding to John's longstanding Jennifer Aniston crush.

He had not thought about Jennifer Aniston once all day, but with Gert he knew how to quit when ahead. In any event, another pretty face had caught his eye. That cute little congressgirl from New York who was always on. The barmaid with the big mouth. She was definitely out there, but too vacuous to be any real threat to his way of life. John couldn't hate her the way Republicans did; she was too sweet to look at.

He settled on a news channel, waiting for the storm to pass. "On the campaign trail today," reported Anchorwoman in living black and white, "Emily Upton defended herself against charges of corruption. Sarah Mills has the story."

Reporter Mills was on location. "The Upton campaign is still hearing whispers about corruption. Rumors that began in the nineties with the nearly $1 million in profits she made from her trading in corn futures. The windfall coming at a time when her husband, former Senate Majority Leader, Phil Upton, was chairman of the powerful Commodity Futures Trading Commission."

File footage ran of a younger, almost pretty, Emily playing the gender card in giving a perfectly reasonable explanation for her market wizardry. "People question my knowledge of corn futures trading, and they want to weave some sort of conspiracy theory involving my husband." She went on to impeach the small minds and outmoded notions of those who dared disbelieve. "I've been hearing these snide insinuations my entire career—that a woman can't succeed without help from a man. Well, there's nothing that says a woman can't be a shrewd investor. I learned about the commodities markets as a young girl, on the knee of my uncle, Cyrus Rogers, an Indiana corn farmer."

"A *man*." John laughed at having the last word.

Mills continued in voice-over, as John watched today's bloated and blighted Emily waving happily to supporters. "More recent criticism points to million-dollar Wall Street speaking fees, and accusations of influence peddling by the secretary of state. Her critics charge that she and her husband view the Upton Foundation, with its lengthy list of foreign donors, as their personal ATM."

Crabby and hoarse, Emily Upton responded. "Always with the same old distractions while I'm busy fighting for America. My husband and I are proud of the work of our foundation. The right-wing fake news media are reporting that we're worth hundreds of millions of dollars, but I don't concern myself with material reward. I just believe in good old-fashioned hard work."

To which John laughed out loud. "Who says your candidate doesn't have a sense of humor."

Emily Rogers Upton launched into a red-faced—"Water, get her some water!"—coughing fit. The camera cut to Mills, caught in an ironic smirk. "Certainly no one has ever questioned Emily Upton's work ethic, but her Republican rival Jim O'Leary is calling for an independent audit of the Upton Foundation. I'm Sarah Mills."

"The perfect choice to head the free world kleptocracy," John opined.

"And what is that supposed to mean?"

"Except that by the time the Uptons are finished, there won't be anything left for the rest."

"You're unbalanced."

He was going to town with a back scratcher. Gert moved about the room, armed with a can of Green Bomb cleanser and roll of recycled paper towels, furnished by management. "Tomorrow, it's your turn."

"I'll take out the trash."

"This is *Progress*, John. It's an injustice."

He caught the tail end of an interview with his candidate, Jon Small. The Louisiana congressman, fearless and plainspoken, with a drawl that belied the fire behind it, questioning why a nation that was essentially insolvent continued to send billions of dollars in aid overseas.

"They should be sending us aid."

When informed by his interviewer—a journalist of renown clearly offended by such loose talk—that his call to bring American troops home from various global hot spots would be a threat to vital American interests, the twelve-term legislator asked him to define "American interests." The journalist, a professed foreign policy authority, studied in pomposity, responded with the usual vague, high-flown generalities, couched in patriotic prattle.

"I know," responded Congressman Small, plainly exhausted by the rhetoric, "America's standing in the world, our leadership role, blah-blah-blah. Tell that to the soldier from New Jersey who plays golf today on one leg. Small consolation for the young mom in Kansas, left to care for two little ones, after having lost her husband—and their father—fighting in one of these pointless conflicts. Or endless occupations. Look them in the eye and tell them. And that's not to mention the *millions* of innocents that we, and our faithful allies, have maimed and burned alive."

"Keeping the world safe for plutocracy," John cracked wise.

"The American people have been sold a lie. Here's the answer to my question, Chris," continued the man John knew by rights should be president. "And it's in two parts. American, is short for the American Empire. Interests, the *financial* interests of the major banks, transnational corporations, and the military-industrial-security state—accountable to no one—that drains the lifeblood of this republic. All in the stated aim of spreading democracy. But then," he concluded with a patronizing smile, "we know it's really all about power . . . don't we, Chris."

John swung at a fly with the back scratcher. "Don't look now, but there's a fox in the whorehouse."

"The idea of America as an empire has been thoroughly discredited," spoke the award-winning reporter out of the side of his mouth; a mediocre talent who rode into the business on his father's coattails.

"By whom?" asked the congressman.

"By . . . seasoned observers."

"Well, perhaps your observers should go more heavily on the seasoning. If *eight hundred* American bases in more than a hundred countries does not constitute an empire, I don't know what does. Your big bad bogeymen, the Russians, have bases in three."

The takeaway, by a trusted talking head, and faithful defender of the status quo (like all the rest who know a good gig when they find one), was a rash denunciation of Congressman Small as a dangerous isolationist, who sounded suspiciously like a Russian asset. It was a service to his country (not to mention their own meaningless careers), his corporate cousins at rival networks agreed.

"A CBS News/*New York Times* poll, released today, says that 53 percent of likely voters agree that America is ready for a Hindu president. Alan Winslow reports."

"Buoyed by polls, and encouraged by his widening lead over Democratic rival Emily Upton, Benjamin Jamaal Singh confronted another issue head-on today."

Winslow continued in voice-over as the Ohio senator, sleeves rolled up, doing his man of the people *shtik*, spoke from a handheld microphone. "At a rally in New Jersey, Emily Upton's backyard, he talked about the problem of simmering white rage, and the threat it poses to the integrity of the upcoming election."

"White rage," John harrumphed. "The race baiters are back."

"There is none so blind . . ." said his wife sadly.

". . . as those who don't know bullshit when they step in it."

"The two most serious threats to our national welfare are systemic racism, and the scourge of white nationalism," said the frontrunner. "Extremist groups threaten everything that America holds dear, and a Jamaal Singh administration will not rest until these two cancers are stamped out."

This likely voter wasn't buying it. "We've already had one Black president, and we're about to elect a second. Where is the racism?"

"It's everywhere, John. America's a sewer."

"That's Leslie talking. Do you personally know any racists?"

"I don't associate with their kind."

"Alright, do you know *of* any racists?" When her answer was no answer, John answered for her. "And neither do I."

She lay down next to him with her phone, after an abortive study of her composting brochures. They were boring. She would pass them along to Leslie. She was laughing at videos of mice chasing cats. Apropos, John thought. He waved at several flies before changing to another channel, and the esteemed Mrs. Upton.

"It would be shortsighted, and potentially devastating, to ignore the threat of domestic terrorism and white nationalism to our democracy," the candidate stated. "Neo-Nazi hate groups have infiltrated communities in every corner of America. *This is our most serious threat since the Civil War.* We must be vigilant in defending our way of life against these monsters."

John was scratching his head. "I never heard of this threat till about ten minutes ago."

"Your whiteness is on display . . . and it's *not* a pretty sight."

"I don't even know what that means."

"Totally out of touch. Just like Leslie says." She wasn't sure how well the incremental approach was working.

"Leslie's intelligence network. What's she reporting? Neo-Nazis massing along Georgia Avenue?"

"Give them time."

"How about mostly peaceful protests? You know, the kind where they loot all the evil capitalists, and then burn what's left to the ground?"

She didn't answer.

"No? Have the evil white supremacists blown anything up?"

"They're mobilizing." Of all people, her husband should know this. He was the conspiracy theorist.

"You would think they would have shown themselves by now."

"They operate *underground*. Don't you know anything?"

"Has the distinguished team at NBC been able to name any of these groups?"

"They're secret, John."

"The FBI's fingerprints are all over this. Of that, you can be sure."

"There you go with your conspiracy theories."

"There's nothing theoretical about it," he made clear.

"I saw a swastika sprayed on an overpass the other day." So *there*.

"When I actually see these characters, with my own two eyes, goose-stepping their way down 16th Street, I'll believe it."

She had moved on to a how-to on balloon sculptures. Put off by the blather, John jumped to another channel—and Republican Jim O'Leary.

"The intelligence agencies warn it's not the external threats posed by Russia or China, but racism and radical white nationalism that are the gravest threats to our nation's security. The danger within."

"What about your buddy Putin, there, Senator Maverick?"

"Until we come together as Americans—black, white, and brown, and make the tough choices—"

"Ain't democracy grand." John laughed in derision, turning off the TV. "They're all in on it."

He rolled out of bed and rolled up his magazine. "The moralizers divide us every which way they can. Then, when all hell breaks loose, they look *shocked*."

Gert was on Leslie's Facebook page, not liking photos posted by Leslie's Republican friend Alison; the one Gert couldn't stand. Like Leslie was making inroads. They had money was what it was, and lord knows Leslie loved being around money. Alison and her xenophobic husband had just returned from two to-die-for weeks in Bermuda with their three perfect children. Second thoughts about vacation choices crossed Gert's mind—dismissed out of hand.

John advanced from table, to dresser, to chair in his boxers, taking out flies.

"What are you doing, John?"

Whack! "Making tough choices."

"And what do you expect to do with the dead flies?"

"Throw them in the trash. Where they belong." *Whack!* Missed.

"What if she checks the trash?"

Whack! "Alright, I'll throw them in the compost."

"You will not."

He scooped up remains, and headed for the bathroom; and burial at sea. She heard the flush.

"So how do we explain the missing flies?"

He reappeared. "Have you completely lost your mind?"

In Phase II, he went from corner to corner collecting the boxes of mouse food, before disappearing again into the bathroom. She heard another flush.

As he emerged from the bathroom, a lone mouse scurried by. "Yeah. Go feed in someone else's room!" The mad avenger turned on his wife. She had never seen him like this. "You know, there's a difference between wildlife, and vermin."

"Get ahold of yourself, John."

"What about the poor roaches? Why should they go hungry?"

He was on a rampage. Their happy vacation in jeopardy, Gert put her phone aside and rose to engage. "The flies. The mouse food. She could have us thrown out of here."

"Please."

He threw his stupid magazine in the compost.

"That goes in paper, John."

CHAPTER 10

Gert wasn't feeling well.

"What's wrong?" sympathetic husband asked.

"I don't *feel* well, John."

No accounting of symptoms would be forthcoming, though there were indications her sad state was the product of her intemperate husband's meltdown from the previous evening. What John *knew*, was that nobody did sick like his wife. She lay in bed, moaning. He moved in close.

"Is it your head?"

"Get away from me."

But for the balance of the morning, her utterances rose barely above the whispers of one on the brink—blank stare fixed on the opposing wall. Should he call for a priest?

"You're a jerk."

"Did you take your medication?"

She glared at him—with contempt that bordered on loathing. "I already told you. I'm *out* of my medication."

He had been dispatched to the Progress Pharmacy for a refill, slipping out the back to evade a certain keeper of a certain inn. The pharmacy—such as it was—on Elm Street, just around the corner from justice patrol headquarters. It was eerie walking down aisles lined with empty shelves. Alas, they were out of Gert's medication.

"Did you get my Tylenol? I only have three left."

"You didn't say anything about Tylenol."

"You don't care about anyone but yourself."

He tried to make light of the situation. "You're going to miss the workshop," he said, glint in his eye.

"I wouldn't be caught dead at that burlesque show."

An emergency call was placed long-distance to Dr. Spillman, whose PA had instructed the patient to rest and drink plenty of fluids. These kept her in the bathroom much of the day. The rest was occupied with sleeping, among her singular talents. For John, this a delicious respite from the carping; how his sour disposition was ruining a perfectly wonderful vacation.

With Gert laid up, he was left to his own devices. What the hell was there to do anyway in that goofy town? His natural inclination would have been to hide out in their room, but there was nothing to watch on TV, and he had already finished his book. He had paid for it twice; he didn't feel like reading it twice. The prospect of a day's confinement with an ailing she-bear was grisly. He thought about the Octavia show—but *she* was sure to find out—and he was in deep enough already. He wondered if Progress had a library.

# # #

"I'm so sorry to hear about Mrs. Smith. How is she feeling?"

The walls had ears. "Not too good, Mrs. Gilroy."

The mayor and keeper of the inn had her own issues. An ugly rumor had been circulating for months—and finally the county zoning commission had made it official—approving a massive site just outside borough limits for the construction of a new Walmart.

"What will this do to the character of our community?"

"Is it within cycling distance?"

"And what effect will it have on our merchants, Mr. Smith?" she pleaded.

Judging from that pharmacy, the local merchants were underwater already. "They serve niche markets," he said reassuringly.

"This simply goes against all that Progress stands for."

Like *progress*, John thought. But he actually felt for this sorry pied piper and her little menagerie. As long as they weren't hurting anybody, there was still a place in the world for the bohemian, the eccentric, and the utopians to live out their days in peace. Or there should be. And Mrs. Gilroy was quite harmless, he had come to realize.

"I'm sorry to hear that." And he was. Consolidation and corporatization were stripping life of its romance.

After wiping away a single tear, she put on a smile, and asked John if he was ready for Giving Tuesday.

"I'm not really familiar with that one, Mrs. Gilroy."

"One day out of the week is our chance to give back, Mr. Smith. Will you join us?"

When he hesitated, she was ready with suggestions. "Well, let's see. We already have your generous donation to GALS, but they are certainly in need of more. Contributions are down," she said sadly. "And there's always Save The Worm! The Pacific spotted milkworm, that is. The committee has had to scale back some of their life-affirming efforts due to a lack of funding."

She had more. "Perhaps the Portable Toilet Fund, in support of our residents currently experiencing homelessness. They deserve comfortable facilities, and frankly," she added discreetly, lest she be exposed and thrown to the mob, "that would benefit us *all*."

"Altruism goes both ways, Mrs. Gilroy."

Abruptly she slapped the counter. "How could it have escaped me? The Gender Studies Center! And I didn't realize the time, Mr. Smith, but you're late for today's workshop."

"I don't think I can make the workshop today. Maybe tomorrow."

"Oh, dear. Octavia will be so disappointed. You had said you would." She chewed her lip. "Do you have sons, Mr. Smith?"

"Why, yes. We have two."

"Then it's imperative that you make part two of today's session: Why Your Son *Should* Play with Dolls."

"Well, they're grown, Mrs. Gilroy. It would be their decision."

"And they seem at home in the gender roles they've chosen? I trust you allowed them to make the decision for themselves."

"I think hormones played a part."

"Our poor children."

"I second that." He looked at his watch. "Mrs. Gilroy, I'm keeping you."

"Not at all, Mr. Smith. We enjoy your company. Can I put you down for a donation to the center?"

"Let me talk it over with my wife. By the way, does Progress have a library?"

"We certainly do!" she said with reflexive pride, before her countenance drooped. "Unfortunately, they've been forced to downsize, temporarily, due to a budget shortfall."

\# \# \#

John had forgotten about the resistance. They had massed bright and early across the way, awaiting his appearance. He was able to count eleven cellulite-dinted, white-cake asses mooning him. Where was the diversity? The male standard bearer—what *was* his story anyway?—carried a sign reading: WALMART IS *NOT* PROGRESS!

John wanted to tell them he wanted no part of Walmart. He was old-school brick and mortar, but he didn't shop there.

The remaining three ladies made it unanimous, and under threatening skies, fourteen naked women and a lone fully dressed male—#metoo dictates no doubt at play—serenaded John from one side of Main Street, as he made his way down the other.

> "Racist, sexist, homophobe,
> Go back on the horse you rode.
> Racist, sexist, homophobe,
> Go back on the horse you rode."

Not exactly proper rhyme, but John didn't want to add flame to smolder. The poor guy must be dying, presuming he was not of nuanced gender, that much booty within reach.

A cluster of supporters followed, jeering at John, if not sure why. The typical refrain from conservatives regarding activists—"Don't these people have jobs?"—made John wonder where the jobs *were* in Progress. Nobody seemed to do much of anything. With nudity apparently no bar to family-friendly amusement. Did they have schools there? Might there be a fourth-grade teacher in the assemblage? "Look, it's Ms. Kilgallen!" Heaven knows what a Ms. Kilgallen must be teaching those kids.

Remembering his empty wallet, he stopped at Progress Federal for some cash—but was told they were out. Some bank.

The Tom Hayden Library lived down to expectations. The elderly little librarian in rainbow sweater and pin sweetly apologized to John, explaining that due to budget cuts the library had been reduced to three sections: Political Thought, Children's Fiction, and Barack Obama.

The Political Thought section would prove interesting. John found both sides represented: socialist *and* utopian. The writings of Julian Huxley and H.G. Wells bookended Marx and Trotsky. Nietzsche. Jean-Jacques Rousseau. There was Draco, and his model for today's Borough of Progress. Having renounced conservatism in favor of a more libertarian perspective, John was not afraid to delve. Naomi Wolf, Noam Chomsky, and Chris Hedges were liberal thinkers who deserved to be heard. And there was Camille Paglia, another of John's favorites. The curators were to be commended for their extensive collections of the works of George Bernard Shaw and Bertrand Russell; men with whom John found little common ground—a Fabian socialist and a eugenicist—but as the notorious free thinkers of their day, historical personalities of note.

There they were. A dozen copies of *Earth in The Balance*. A half dozen *Rules for Radicals*. John wondered if a single reader had ever made it through all three volumes of *Jerry Brown: A Life*. There was *The Sellout* by a Dr. Felix Runkel, on the life and times of Jerry Rubin, and his conversion to capitalist. John Maynard Keynes was all there was to know about economics. Murray Rothbard? Heavens! He doubted that Mrs. Gilroy, or anyone else in Progress for that matter, had ever heard of H.L. Mencken.

John had always liked biographies. He applied for a temporary card and selected one on Russell, to go with Chomsky's *Manufacturing Consent*. With nothing else to do, he headed for Children's Fiction. Eight years was enough Barack Obama. Through the front window, he saw that the heavens had opened. *Sober White Male* held picket sign in one hand, umbrella in the other, while his merry *compatriettes* danced in the rain—precluded from joining in the frivolity for fear of inadvertently violating a body part.

A book with a cute little cow on the cover, all long lashes and cowbell, caught his eye. *Meet Elsie* by a Jo Gustafson. John read up on Ms. Gustafson, a former diesel mechanic who had dropped the "e" when she transitioned ten years before. Judging by the square-jawed visage on the inside back flap, this was one children's author to be reckoned with.

As a young bull, Ellsworth had always questioned his identity. He'd known from very young that he was different. He would wink at the other growing bulls—who all thought he was weird. When they would hang out in the corner of the barnyard, eyeballing the heifers and talking dirty, he felt left out of the conversation. He liked his playmates as more than friends, but was terrified of telling them. Word got around to stay away from Ellsworth.

The heifers accepted him. He loved how they could pee out the back. It was like a golden waterfall. He giggled like one of the girls when they argued about which of the bulls was the cutest. Ellsworth had his own favorite, a young longhorn named Tex. When they dreamed about becoming mommies someday, Ellsworth fantasized about giving birth to a little one of his very own.

One afternoon Mabel, the old mother cow, caught Ellsworth moping in the shade of the big ole apple tree, while the others frolicked in the sun.

"What's the matter, Ellsworth?" she asked.

"I don't know, Miss Mabel. I just don't fit in."

Wise old Mabel listened to Ellsworth's story. "Did you ever tell this to your mother?"

"Oh no, Miss Mabel. I could never tell my mother." But he could talk to Mabel. He told her how he wanted to be pretty, and wear a shiny cowbell, just like hers.

"I can do something about the cowbell," she assured him. As for the rest, "Mean old Farmer McGee will be coming around any day now with his razor blade. The other boys hate it, but for you, Ellsworth, it will be the day your dreams come true."

Old Mabel was right. It hurt for a time, but while the gang lay around the barnyard licking their wounds, and plotting death to Farmer McGee, Ellsworth was happier than he ever could have imagined. Wise old Mabel told him he could be whoever he wanted, if it was in his heart. He couldn't have a baby of his own—Farmer McGee would never go for the surgery— but he could still adopt. Ellsworth said he liked that. And he liked the new name Mabel had given him: *Elsie*.

John turned the book over. "Brings a tear to the eye. A triumph of the bovine spirit," hailed *The New York Times*.

"A tour de force! Questioning children the world over will be emboldened by Elsie, and her story of affirmation," proclaimed *The San Francisco Examiner*.

"There's an Elsie inside all of us, waiting to come out," wrote *The Village Voice*."

The Village Voice?

\# \# \#

This should be good, John thought, pulling *Wilma Goes to Washington* from the shelf. Wilma was a self-willed little girl with freckles and pigtails, and a social conscience way beyond her years.

Wilma was from Wilcox, a small town in the state of Washington. One chilly morning, nine-year-old Wilma looked on as her father started the family SUV to take her to school. As she watched the exhaust vapor drift to the gray sky, she chastised her father for all of the carbon he was releasing into the atmosphere. Her father said he didn't know any other way of doing it. Spunky little Wilma informed her father—in no uncertain terms—that if that was the case, she would ride her bike to school that day. It was far too dangerous, they told her, but feisty little Wilma with the blonde pigtails wasn't having it. "If I was a *boy* you'd let me," she said, gender-shaming her mother and father. They had to admit, she probably had a point.

Wilma rode her bike to school that day; and the day after. There came a time when Wilma informed her parents that, in good conscience, she could no longer ride in the family SUV—until they got an electric vehicle, that is. When her father said they couldn't afford one, Wilma started a GoFundMe page, and was able to raise enough money to buy her family a new Tesla.

Wilma's story was only beginning. She wondered why more people didn't ride bikes instead of cars. Her mother said it was probably because there weren't enough bike lanes.

Wilma had an idea. She would ride her bike to the state capital of Olympia, and petition the governor and the legislature to create more bike lanes. Two local television stations covered Wilma's hundred-mile trip. By the end little Wilma was tired, but the sight of the Capitol dome in the distance had infused her with a new vigor.

The next morning, nine-year-old Wilma Wilson of Wilcox, Washington, addressed the legislature on the ABCs of climate change, and how it would be awesome if everyone rode bikes. After a lunch of bean sprouts and macadamia nuts—like many an aware nine-year-old, Wilma was vegan—she met personally with the governor. The governor promised to work with the legislature to create five hundred miles of new bike lanes. Wilma said why not make it a thousand? That was twice as many, right? The governor smiled and said that would cost a lot of money, and the state was already running something he called a deficit. But he said that maybe they could sell bonds to raise the money. Wilma didn't know what bonds were. Her father said they were pieces of paper that people paid money for, or something like that. Wilma didn't know why they wouldn't do that all the time. It sounded so easy.

The next day the legislature passed Wilma's Law, creating more than a thousand miles of new bicycle lanes throughout the state of Washington. Wilma was a local hero, and she became a favorite of the nice people at the Good News Network. All of America marveled at the insight of a nine-year-old girl.

# # #

John looked up. The resistance was making ghoulish faces at him through the window. Thankfully, they weren't allowed inside the library without towels to sit on. He moved to a different table, and returned to Wilma and her adventures.

# # #

April came. The winter snows had melted, and Wilma was ready to put her grandest plan of all into action. More people were riding bikes—and that was good—but there were still way too many cars and trucks running on what her teacher called fossil fuels. Wilma knew she had to talk to the president. The planet depended on it, and time was running out.

Wilma saved her allowance money, and everyone did fundraisers. When school let out for the summer, Wilma had gotten all A's on her report card. She signed off her *Indigenous Peoples Project* podcast for the summer, and with her mother and father following in the family Tesla, took off on her bike the next day. GNN covered every mile of her journey. The people at the Mean News Channel wondered if it was really necessary for this child to ride her bike the entire breadth of the country. Why couldn't she just fly in a plane? The whole thing was ridiculous, they said.

They called it virtue signaling. Wilma was undeterred by the people her mother and father called *skeptics*. She was a change agent.

Through rains and searing heat, Wilma pedaled. Fortunately, she had a tail wind most of the way. It was still a hard trip. She had a flat tire in Wyoming, and another in Nebraska. Wilma fixed them herself. Her dad had offered to help, but she told him he was being sexist. One of her pedals broke off outside Kansas City, and in St. Louis the bicycle itself had collapsed from metal fatigue. Wilma was in tears, but the Sierra Club came to the rescue, wiring her parents the money for a new one.

She liked her new bike. It had gears. They made her go faster. She was nearing West Virginia, and the mountains. Everyone said it would be easier if she went around through Pennsylvania, but Wilma said no mountain was going to stop a girl who was empowered. In her nightly GNN interview, she admitted she did have to get off her bike and push sometimes.

Pigtails flying, America's sweetheart raced down Pennsylvania Avenue. President Goodwell was waiting to greet her, along with a bunch of people with cameras. He was a nice man, and his wife, Mrs. Goodwell, was pretty—even though Wilma knew in her heart that strong women were more than sex objects. They gave Wilma a tour of the White House. Her teacher, Ms. Honeycutt, had said that President Goodwell was only the second African American president. Wilma said that wasn't fair. Ms. Honeycutt explained that America was a bad country, full of people who didn't want to vote for somebody who looked different. That made Wilma sad.

Wilma and her parents spent the night in the Lincoln Bedroom. The next day, she and President Goodwell met in the Oval Office. The key to her Green Fourteen Points, Wilma told the president, was that with climate change and all, it would be better if everyone drove electric cars. The president agreed, but said it would take time to get the whole country to change its ways. Wilma thought two years sounded about right, and the president said that would be a good goal. The car companies said that would be hard, and cost a lot of money. Wilma asked what was more important—money—or the planet? The president and the people on TV said Wilma was wise beyond her years.

Everyone, that is, except the people at the Mean News Channel. They called Wilma Wilson's Green Fourteen Points a little girl's pipe dream, and complained about something they called fiscal lunacy. They said forcing everybody to drive electric vehicles would bankrupt the country. And why were we listening to a nine-year-old anyway? President Goodwell told Wilma not to feel bad; the Mean News Channel didn't like him either.

The next day they said goodbye to President and Mrs. Goodwell, threw Wilma's bike in the back of the Tesla, and drove home to a parade in her honor. ABC News made her their Person of the Week! for making a difference, even though her Green Fourteen Points never made it to committee. Everyone said she might be the first woman president, but Wilma only wanted to be the second. After Emily Upton. Everybody laughed, and cheered, and cried.

John read *Wilma Goes to Washington* cover to cover. By the end, he was exhausted.

# # #

John found his wife asleep, snoring to beat the band. He had returned from the Tom Hayden Library unmolested; the resistance having gone home to dry off, lest they catch their death of cold. Even fire-breathing anti-fascists had to listen to their bodies.

She was stirring. "Do you have to make so much noise?"

"I tried to be quiet."

"Why are you all wet?"

"Because . . . it's raining?" He kicked off wet shoes. "Nobody in this town bothers with umbrellas. I asked Mrs. Gilroy where I could find one, and she looked at me like I was speaking Gaelic."

"Where did you go?"

"To the library." As he changed into dry clothes, he asked if she was hungry.

"I don't *feel* well, John."

\#   \#   \#

In the end, Gert had decided her condition could only improve with a good vegan meal. They had, for the moment, escaped the rain in the shelter of the canopy fronting Mi Hong's Shanghai Shack. The notice from the Borough of Progress Health Department was posted inside the front door: Closed Due to Dietary Violations.

"Wow. The regulatory arm works fast around here."

"He was warned."

"I was hoping I might chance upon some dead cow flesh in my lo mein," he said, mouth watering.

"I'm hungry, John."

"The problem is, I walked the three blocks to the library, and this was the only place still in business."

Back in their room, they munched on granola bars from The Mildred McFadden Pavilion; neither, as yet, ready to brave another meal from the Deegan Vegan.

"These aren't bad," he said, pleasantly surprised.

"They're upsetting my stomach," said his wife.

CHAPTER 11

Crazy Woman

Gert's recovery had been nothing short of miraculous. The sight of her all decked out in pink was a rude awakening. John stretched and sat up in bed, watching her pin the pink bow to her hair.

"Feeling better?"

"I feel wonderful!" she said to the mirror.

"What's with the getup?"

"Today is Pink-Out, John."

Look at her. All put out. Through an extended yawn he wondered, did she really expect him to keep up with all this female stuff?

"A sorry expression of indifference, to your wife . . . and to those of her downtrodden gender." And to think he had referred to poor Millie as a hopeless case. "No matter, I've laid out your ribbon."

A strip of pink ribbon John estimated at a foot in length stretched across his dresser.

"I don't wear ribbons."

"You will today."

"Uh, I will not."

"Well then, I guess I'll be going to the beach by myself."

"Watch out for riptides." He picked up his Noam Chomsky and opened to where he had left off the night before.

"You're incorrigible."

"I beseech thy mercy, O illumined one." He considered for a moment. "I volunteered to attend your woke workshop, in case you've forgotten." Visions of the comely Octavia blazed before him.

"I will not deliver my husband to the clutches of that harlot."

He climbed out of bed, headed for the bathroom. She continued with her primping and preening. When he came back out—

"There's no hot water."

"I noticed that." She held the ribbon, tied in a neat bow. "You can pin this to your hat. It won't hurt a bit."

He took it, and ambled over to the bins. "Does this go in trash, or is it recyclable?"

She took it back and put it in her purse. "You're going to put it on. Now, or later."

# # #

"It's so good to see you up and about, Mrs. Smith."

Did this woman never sleep? And, yet, she was always so chipper. The indomitable spirit of the zealot. That's what John needed more of in his life. Zeal.

"I'm feeling so much better today, thank you, Mrs. Gilroy."

"I had a touch of the same thing just this past week."

A touch of *what*? Between the two of them they were hurting his eyes. Like dueling bottles of Pepto Bismol. The mayor's white Alpine hat with pink feather perfectly suited to an altogether farcical persona. Where did she find such trifles?

"You're obviously in the spirit, Mrs. Smith."

Mrs. Gilroy turned her attention to the recalcitrant *Mister* Smith, the closest thing to pink on his person the orange bill of that unsightly baseball cap. A childish expression of virility, and the male preoccupation with territory. "Won't you be joining us for Pink-Out, Mr. Smith?"

"Why am I being coerced into wearing a color that doesn't suit me, Mrs. Gilroy?"

"Mr. Smith, the wearing of the color pink is the universal symbol of woman's struggle against breast cancer."

"Do you have any other disease days?"

After a moment, and with a quizzical expression, she responded, "I'm not sure I follow, Mr. Smith."

"You know, like a *Blue-Out* for prostate cancer? Men get sick too."

She was beginning to get an idea of what poor Mrs. Smith must go through. "Well, women—"

"What will my wearing that sissy bow do to improve the situation?"

"It raises awareness Mr. Smith . . . to the worthy cause of breast cancer research . . . and the oppression of women in general."

"An empty gesture, in other words."

"Certainly not. It demonstrates caring, and empathy."

"I don't know, Mrs. Gilroy. You have the babies, but we already *die* younger than you. We're the ones who dig the ditches, plow the fields, shovel the snow, tote the barges, and fight the wars. You women seem to be doing well enough without my ribbon in the game."

Through the front window he could see the resistance, lined up like so many pink flamingos. "Who are they?"

"They," said the mayor emphatically, "are the Conscience of Progress— embodying the activist spirit for which we are known."

"They seem to be singling me out."

"Perhaps that's your guilty conscience talking, Mr. Smith."

"It's like living with a rock, Mrs. Gilroy."

# # #

They stepped from the office, to a tinderbox. The women of the Conscience, gathering followers, were outfitted for confrontation in pink slacks, sweat-shirts, and beanies—crowned by tumescent plastic nipples. The thoroughgoing emasculation of Sensitive White Male in evidence the moment he slipped his on. The beard would probably go next. His wardrobe bereft of anything pink (a sign of latent homophobia the women agreed), the best he could contribute moving forward, a pair of pink Nikes, recently purchased.

> "Racist, sexist, homophobe,
> Go back on the horse you rode.
> Racist, sexist, homophobe,
> Go back on the horse you rode."

So it went—

> "Racist, sexist, homophobe,
> Go back on the horse you rode.
> Racist, sexist, homophobe,
> Go back on the horse you rode."

A strange something stirred in Gert. She was moved to defend her husband. "My husband is not a racist!" she shouted.

"He's a *rapist*," the vocal leader responded. "You're married to a rapist! *YOU'RE ALL RAPISTS!*"—her primal shriek underscored by a frantic pumping of little fists, and stomping of feet.

Knowing he hadn't made a move on his wife in years, John waited for an answer, but Gert saw she was no match for this one.

> "*Rapist*, sexist, homophobe,
> Go back on the horse you rode.
> *Rapist*, sexist, homophobe,
> Go back on the horse you rode."

"I can feel the empathy."

"It's karma, John."

"You're a *rapist!*" shouted Sensitive White Male, of a piece.

What the hell was this guy's story? In John's view—and to the extent that he regarded gender as a matter worthy of even five seconds of his or any other thinking individual's consideration—this dude should do the only decent and honorable thing, and surrender his testicles to the authorities.

Crazy Woman was John's principal suspect in the bra attack. She seemed to be the brains of the operation. To that point they had kept to the far side of the street. How long before empathy boiled over?

"Take your white privilege and go home!" she screamed; although the happy messenger gave every indication of being, herself, white. This, again, calling to mind the startling lack of diversity; an unwritten principle being at work. White liberals, as our moral superiors, and possessed of perfect knowledge, not generally required to actually *practice* what they preach. John was willing to give this sampling the benefit of the doubt, though, knowing diversity came in many stripes.

"You think we're all just a bunch of queers, don't you?" shouted one, who was actually kind of cute, in the binary sense. Like his wife, able to read his mind. From across the street, no less. He speculated at the diversity of thought in this charming little coterie.

"What we do in our bedrooms is none of your business," she amended—with Fourth Amendment fervor. "What kind of example are you setting for your daughter, you pig?"

John was prepared to answer that, at the moment, he was relieved not to have a daughter.

"I'm trans," cried another, "and the three of us are lovers," she broadcast, linking arms in solidarity with a similarly androgynous pair. "Make something of that!"

Now *there* was a modern family. Rental bikes with helmets waited. Gert hung her carry bag on the handlebars and saddled up. John passed on the helmet. By local ordinance all bicycles in Progress were to be gender neutral. Gert had an unfamiliar bar to contend with, but John said not a word. The PC movement, in time, he believed, would eat itself.

"Where's your pink?" Crazy Woman demanded of John.

"Yeah, where's your pink, asshole?" sneered Sensitive White Male.

"*These mean nothing to you?*" Crazy Woman wailed, yanking up her sweatshirt, where twin soft appendages hung on for dear life. Poor kid. She really shouldn't be throwing bras around.

Gert produced John's pink bow. To her surprise he stepped from his bike and took it with a flourish—but to her horror threw *down* the gauntlet—grinding it into Main Street with the sole of his white New Balance. There.

In the high court of tolerance, this was an act of aggression that would not stand. With the butt end of his WOMEN RULE! placard Sensitive White Male smashed the front window of Jackie and Jill's Bakery;

forgetting that the proprietors were two women, prominent in the local LGBT community.

"Now you did it, John."

They took off on their bikes under a fusillade of organic bagels—baked fresh daily. These proved the perfect weapon, aerodynamic, with mass sufficient to travel impressive distances thrown with the proper spiral. The Conscience scooped up as many as they could and gave chase helter-skelter, firing at will.

"Stop right there!" Officer McCoy had pulled up on her replacement bike as the pursued reached the church.

"We received a call about a disturbance," the officer announced, battling a stubborn kickstand. Though shorter by a foot, she managed nonetheless to look down her nose at John. "We figured you must be involved."

"They were attacking us, Officer McCoy," Gert gave witness.

"And it's not the first time," John added.

"*You* be quiet." She whipped out her ticket book. "ID."

With the arrival of authority, the Conscience had pulled up short.

"Excuse me, Officer McCoy, but what—"

"To start with, Mr. Smith," the officer interrupted, "you were operating a two-wheeled vehicle without the appropriate head protection."

The toy siren signaled her approach. The Chief, rushing to the scene, mini squad-cart groaning under her bulk—

"Don't you dare laugh, John."

—as it splashed through the puddles, flashing red and blue. She switched off the siren as she pulled to a stop. Looking every inch the cyborg enforcer in full tactical gear, she and her shiny black boots wheeled, and stepped from cart to mud street. She flipped up the plasti-shield visor and removed the gas mask—clipped to her belt for ready redeployment. "Alright, what's going on here?"

Officer McCoy saluted. "Preliminary investigation finds Mr. Smith triggering an uproar, Chief."

"We were assaulted, Chief." They could say what they liked about her husband, she would be implicated as well.

Crazy Woman approached, shouldering up to her elder before being restrained by The Chief. "Pardon me, *ma'am*, but right before our eyes your husband desecrated a symbol sacred to the sisterhood"—in proximity looking more fatuous than ferocious in beanie and nipple.

"Is that true?" The Chief wanted to know.

"Young woman, to exactly whom do you think you are speaking?"

The Conscience of Progress was not accustomed to pushback. And she was not *about* to hear it from this old broad. "To a submissive violet," she sputtered, artfully curtsying, "bowing to the patriarchy." She rose—trembling with rage—chest heaving from the passion of compassion. "You're not fit to wear the color."

The insolence. "Pardon me, you *upstart*, but I burned my first bra before you were born," Gert sallied, advancing on her accuser. "And I will not be rebuked in such fashion by this *infant*," she roundly informed The Chief.

"I don't recall anyone asking for your two cents, Granny."

Gert drew back her bag—ready for the haymaker—before the arm of the law came between them. "And for your information, you *wench*," she jeered, backed off by Officer McCoy, "I know Gloria Steinem *personally*."

"Who?"

"Alright, that's enough," growled The Chief, calling an end to the parley, such as it was. "There will be no cat fights around here today."

"That was a sexist remark, Chief!" Crazy Woman fired back.

"Oh, give it a rest," said The Chief.

# # #

Justice had been served. The Chief, who doubled as magistrate, had presided over a fair and impartial hearing. John was placed on probation for creating a public nuisance, inciting a riot, and misdemeanor insensitivity. As a white cisgender male, with its attendant privileges, he was directed to be respectful of the rights and feelings of those laboring under the weight of intersectionality. When he testified that he didn't know what intersectionality was, he was informed that ignorance of the law was no defense, and that he would be advised to familiarize himself with Progress's Intersectionality Code, recently annotated. A fine of $300 was imposed for the operation of a two-wheeled vehicle without a protective helmet. When he respectfully declined to assist in the subsequent cleanup of baked goods, he was assessed an additional $300 for littering. His petition that a restraining order be placed against the Conscience of Progress was denied. Their First Amendment right to peaceably assemble was not to be infringed without cause.

The Conscience was charged with misdemeanor disturbing the peace. Charges to be dropped, if, and when, restitution was made to the proprietors of Jackie and Jill's. They would appeal.

#   #   #

"You humiliated me, John."

She chose not to speak to him for the first leg of the trip—making for a pleasant ride. Putting the multicultural miasma in the rearview mirror had already put our hero in a better frame of mind. He would Google "cisgender." They left the vagrant encampments behind, and finally reached that area unspoiled by man's influences. Headwinds winnowed the remaining strands atop his head. He had ditched the helmet a mile back but, with the specter of sunburn, had retrieved the Oriole hat from his pocket. From time to time he sneaked a look at his wife—impassive in pink—eyes fixed on the bumpy dirt road that was starting to dry out.

The Oregon countryside welcomed them in living color, with savory bouquet. Rabbit, deer, beaver, and species foreign to John crossed their path. Geese flew overhead, and he thought he saw a wild turkey. The brochure had said they might see buffalo. They entered the pine forest, and the first scent of serenity since they left home. This was going to be a good day.

The trail narrowed, and they continued with caution when it veered steeply downhill.

"John, it's so beautiful!" A conditional pardon had been granted. As an American husband in the modern era, his permanent probationary status understood by all parties to the marital contract.

Dappled in sunshine, the trail was becoming increasingly treacherous, and Gert was struggling. John pulled to the side. "We can walk the rest of the way."

He rested his bike against a tree, and helped Gert off of hers. "Be careful, John. This is a protected area." Only then did he notice the sign: PROTECTED AREA—DO NOT ENTER!—PACIFIC SPOTTED MILKWORM HABITAT.

"What the hell is a Pacific spotted milkworm?"

"The Pacific spotted milkworm is *endangered*, John."

The chasm between man and wife. He was expected to know these things. He did not. Her priorities were not his, and vice versa; paths having diverged eons ago. Man and wife shared a home, and memories, but little else. They rarely agreed, but just as rarely fought. What was the use? She and Leslie probably had a name for such an arrangement. Equipoise? As long he paid the bills and cut the grass, and she kept the house and prepared the meals, the marriage rated as happy.

"So we're not allowed to venture even one foot off the trail?"

"This is their home. How would you like a bunch of strangers traipsing through our home?"

They walked their bikes down the slope. "What makes this worm so special?"

"They play a vital role in the ecosystem, John."

"Maybe not. Maybe they're dying of boredom."

Even walking the bikes was proving difficult. Up ahead, an area had been annexed from the little buggers, with a bench and bike rack.

"Here we are," said Gert.

They parked their bikes in the rack. John wandered over to a wooden stand at the edge of the woods, and the attached plaque: PACIFIC SPOTTED MILKWORM SANCTUARY—OBSERVATION DECK. He climbed the ladder and did a quick look around. "I don't see any worms."

She joined him on the deck. "They're nocturnal, John."

He shrugged and climbed back down. She drank from the arboreal punch for several moments before rejoining him on the ground. "You have no appreciation of nature. Where's your sense of romance?"

They had a seat together in the grass. "I'm very romantic."

There was a heretofore forgotten twinkle in Gert's eye. "You used to be."

He made a study of the treetops before changing the subject. "Cool for June, isn't it?"

"But the sun feels so nice."

He lay down, basking in the warmth. She lay at his side, brown eyes gazing into the azure sky. "Remember all those afternoons on the mall?"

John chuckled. "Frisbees flying overhead."

"You were very romantic back then."

"Mm-hmm. And I almost flunked out, thanks to those sunny afternoons."

"You were so cute, coming to my dorm every night."

"You're all-girl dorm." He laughed. "A guy could screw a girl's brains out—as long as he signed in, and left an ID."

It was more of a giggle, like in days gone by. "You always have had a way of putting things."

"All those trusting fathers sending their little girls off to college. I'm glad we had sons."

She took his hand. "My roommate had the biggest crush on you."

"Mindy?"

"You couldn't tell? The way she laughed at everything you said?" She shook her head. "Oblivious."

Mindy Mandel. Who would have thought? She'd had a great nose job. John had seen the before pictures. He had surprised her naked once—and she had just smiled and said hi. That was pretty cool.

"She was cute. Wish I'd known."

She gave him a little elbow, but still took his hand back. "You did have a thing for the Jewish girls."

They lay there. An idyllic interlude.

"You've been a good husband, John." She took a tremulous breath, tearing up. "And the things you say . . . I'm usually laughing on the inside."

He remembered her from then. Took her in his arms and held her tight, lying there in the grass, in the sunshine.

# # #

They descended the final stretch to the beach, John carrying the bag. The pines reaching almost to the sand; the waves from the blue Pacific breaking on the rocks; the view was spectacular.

"Oh, John!"

He was all smiles, reveling in her jubilation. Washed in negative ions, she spun circles like a little girl. John closed his eyes, buffeted by ocean gusts.

A school of seals relaxed among the rocks, their pups asleep on the sand.

They came to the end of the trail and saw it. Virtually the entire beach was cordoned off. The area prescribed for use by visiting land mammals—the deplorables—a ribbon, barely fifty feet in width, that ran from the base of the trail to the water. The chaste fin and flipper crowd, as birthright, claimed the remainder of a sizable ocean. Lifeguards posted on either side of the ropes served as border patrol agents. Large signs warned: MARINE PROTECTED AREA—DO NOT ENTER!

The strip was a virtual sea of humanity; bathers laid out like so many sardines in a can. John and Gert took it all in, mouths agape. Lines of buoys extended into the sea. Children splashed in the watery confines, lifeguards ready with their whistles should any stray and upset the aquatic balance.

Gert pointed to a spot. They stripped down to their modest swimsuits and did the sunscreen ritual. Choking on pungent second-hand smoke, they tiptoed through a veritable carpet of flesh, bone, and spandex. Signs were posted leading down to the water:

> CANNABIS SMOKING ONLY!!
> NO FOOD OR DRINK!
> NO ALCOHOLIC BEVERAGES!
> PLEASE DO NOT FEED THE SEALS!
> NO SURFING!
> INSURANCE REGULATIONS PROHIBIT DANCING!
> ENJOY YOUR DAY!

They came to what had the makings of a spot. John did the calculus. For them to lie side by side would necessitate mass reconfiguration. "Maybe if we lie in a T."

Gert pulled a couple of beach towels from her bag. They laid them down, careful not to disturb the neighbors.

"Excuse me," said John.

"I'm sorry," apologized Gert.

He lay down gingerly—"Excuse me"—forming the stem.

She lay at his head—"I'm so sorry"—crossing the T.

They were finally free to stretch out. "Ahh . . . this isn't so bad, John."

There was no reply.

"Are you relaxing?"

The wind whistled; the surf roared; seagulls called.

"John?"

CHAPTER 12

A Successful Professional Couple from Chicago

"The honeymooners have returned!"

Some time past sunset, John held the door open for Gert, who looked on the verge of collapse.

"You two made a day of it. Did you not love our beach?"

"What there was of it," said John.

"It was terrible, Mrs. Gilroy."

"Oh?" To this point the keeper of the inn heedless of her favorite guest's infirmity.

Too weak for discourse, that guest left it to her husband. "Our bikes were stolen, and we had to walk all the way back, Mrs. Gilroy."

"Oh, I'm so sorry . . . I'm sure the bikes will turn up."

"I'm exhausted."

"If not, you can pay for them when you check out." Business being business.

"How far was it, John?" inquired the broken-down wreck braced by the front desk.

He had a look at his watch. "It took almost four hours."

"So, you must have passed through our world famous Pacific Spotted Milkworm Sanctuary!"

"Yes . . . we did, Mrs. Gilroy," Gert moaned.

"We're most encouraged. The numbers are on the rise."

"That's very nice, but you know, all I want right now is a nice hot bath."

Their hostess affected an air of heartfelt condolence. "Oh, dear. I'm afraid that won't be possible."

"For heaven's sake, why not?" John had had about enough for one day.

Mrs. Gilroy turned to Gert. "Mrs. Smith, I'm sure you'll understand that in a collective effort to reduce greenhouse emissions, our visitors agree, voluntarily, to forgo hot water on Sundays and Wednesdays. It's on page four of the registration form you signed, Mr. Smith."

"*That* is the most ridiculous thing I've ever heard."

Their indefatigable defender of land, sea, air, and gender autonomy had a practical side. "Oh no, Mr. Smith. It's worked very well. Our energy use is down almost eight percent." All the better for the bottom line.

"What about my wife?"

The mayor appealed to her friend and fellow traveler. "Mrs. Smith, a cold shower can be most invigorating. It will bring you right back. Once attuned, our guests often find they prefer the cold showers. A healthy body, mind, and planet!" Her eyes were brilliant.

"That's alright, Mrs. Gilroy." Head bowed, she and John started for their room.

"Oh, by the way . . ." With nothing short of herculean effort, the proprietress succeeded in dragging John's clubs around from behind the desk. Fresh out of breath, she managed to pant, "These arrived today."

Gert brightened. "Oh good, John. Now you can play."

"I guess people enjoy that sort of thing," their hostess muttered, mopping her brow to great effect.

After confirming the intact arrival of all fourteen clubs, John slung the bag over his shoulder. He studied the portrait of the wild-eyed Mister Gilroy. "What's his story?"

The good mayor was wistful at the mention of her long-departed husband. "I'm afraid our *Mister* Gilroy found himself unable to cope with a changing world." She spoke as if in admonition, to, or at, the figure in the portrait.

"The poor soul . . ."

"Excuse me?"

"I didn't say anything."

"As His Most High Excellency, the Dalai Lama says, 'Anger or hatred is like a fisherman's hook. It is very important for us to ensure that we are not caught by it.'"

"Words we can all live by, Mrs. Gilroy."

"Where is he?" Gert asked softly.

The one left to fend for herself upon life's shifting sands gazed into the distance beyond the front window—and the crossroads of inglorious past, dubious present, and uncertain future.

"There's a most adequate facility, just down the road, that takes very good care of our Mister Gilroy.

# # #

After two days subsisting on granola bars, the vacationers had elected to give the cafe another try, and were surprised to see it half-filled.

Brittany was smiling like all California as she wrote on her pad. "The tofu primavera is a-*may*-zing, Mrs. Smith. You're going to love it."

Gert responded primly. "Thank you." This girl had better watch it.

John was still studying his menu. "Brittany, what exactly is in this mock bacon?"

Brittany loved the stories behind her delicacies. "The mock bacon is Yuba, which is a soy-based meat analog, made by layering the thin skin that forms on the top of boiled soy milk. It's amazing."

In utter despondence, John tossed his menu to the table. "I guess I'll go with the oat bran spaghetti and spicy tofu balls."

"Awwwe-some," said Brittany as she wrote. "That's whole grain. Rich in fiber."

"I can skip the Metamucel tonight."

"You can what?"

"Never mind."

Boomer stuff, she surmised, taking their menus.

# # #

"How long does it take to throw together this slop?"

He glanced in the direction of the kitchen, and back at his watch. It had been at least twenty minutes. "It's not as if there's a line reaching out the door." He looked across at Gert. "You seem to be feeling better."

"Leslie's twenty-minute power nap works wonders."

"You know, I'd almost forgotten about Leslie. The real world seems so far away." He clarified, "Not that there's much of anything real in her world either."

Brittany hopped from table to table, and to and from the kitchen, somehow managing to look busy without actually serving anybody.

At last, dinner came with a smile. "Enjoy in good health."

Gert began eating, but John just stared at his. "How many more days are we here?"

"We need to make the most of every day, John."

"How's yours?"

After four days she could drop the pretense. "Aah."

John looked about for prying eyes, before fishing into his pocket and producing five salt packets. Furtively he tore one open, and began salting his food. Gert leaned toward him. "Where did you get those?" she whispered.

He checked around again before answering. "Remember that guy on the corner?" He sampled his spaghetti before opening a second packet, emptying it as he spoke. "Twenty bucks."

Gert surveyed the room. Sure enough, the other patrons, to a one, gaping at screens. She spoke from behind her napkin. "Can I have one?"

He slid one over to her.

"Should I?"

"I'm sure it could use it."

After further looks around, she opened the packet and salted her food with her right hand, shielding the crime from view with the napkin in her left. Not sure what to do with the empty packet, she rolled it into a ball . . . and slyly dropped it down her blouse. Breathing easier now, she had another taste of her tofu primavera.

"Oh, this is much better." She took on a naughty grin. "I feel so *bad*."

# # #

John was feeling like a new man after his shower, cold though it may have been. Mindy Mandel memories had warmed him up nicely, thank you. Gert had wondered about the length of the shower, but John had pronounced himself ready for more just like it. Her husband was a puzzle.

That husband was half-watching *Tough Customers* as he practiced putting across the worn carpet to the ceramic cup from the bathroom; plastics verboten in this locus of wokeness. Gert had managed to find the

Real Estate Channel on the little TV. In that night's episode, a successful professional couple from Chicago was looking to relocate to Southern California to retire. On at least that much they could agree. John was finding hating this pair a pleasant diversion. The preoccupation with career he had always found irksome, but boring people dug it. Careerists are, as they are *seen*; John self-contained.

Things annoyed John. Accents being one. The foul doctor excepted, New York was suitable to men, obtrusive on women. Chicago accents, as with Southern, were cute on the right woman. This, was not she. She carried way too many pounds for that geometric hairdo John could tell she thought was hot—but that even Jennifer Aniston on her best day would have a hard time pulling off. Did these people not have mirrors? The false eyelashes provided shade on a warm afternoon. Her dweeb husband colored his combover. Even in black and white you could tell. Sad. He, John, had committed to aging gracefully. The guy's glasses were the ones all the fashion slaves were wearing, but it didn't make them any less ugly. That was hard enough for poor John, but they were crooked. And not just crooked. *Crooked.* In *degrees.* Could not his wife, or a producer, or *somebody* please tell the putz to fix the damn glasses?

She wanted Newport Beach; he was sold on San Diego. They had come together at San Clemente, at least for now. He wanted a pool; she didn't. He wanted a two-car garage; she wanted a big yard for their German shepherd to police. She wanted to be able to walk to the beach; ocean air inflamed his sinuses. They agreed on a mud room, until their host politely explained that they don't have mud rooms in Southern California because there's no mud.

And no basements. This was an unwelcome bit of news. Why not? The host didn't know. After five minutes of excruciating back and forth, that maybe Florida would be a better fit for them and their active lifestyle, they agreed, with reservations, to move forward.

They both loved the first house. It was roomy, with a big garage and pool, and it was comfortably under budget in a great location. The realtor host was ready with the papers, but when something seems too good to be true, it usually is.

"The yard's not big enough for Trooper," the wife whined.

On to house number two. She loved the yard, but the downstairs was not open enough. As fashion-forward professionals they loved to entertain, and she required an open concept. John wondered who in his right mind would want to spend an evening with these two.

House number three was a winner, but it was $15,000 over budget. When told the price was firm, CPA husband explained, from behind glasses gone awry, that they could not go that far over budget.

Number four, in Dana Point now, was too far from the beach. The next had a dog park within walking distance, but there was no garage.

Gert wasn't even watching her own show. She sat on the edge of the bed—phone to ear—speaking over the sound of crying. "All this crying doesn't help either, Millie."

Between putts, John could hear gulping sobs.

"If you would stop getting drunk . . . and spreading your legs for your therapists . . . maybe Ted would come back."

The crying stopped. Gert looked at the phone. "She hung up." In a dyspeptic outburst not uncommon to sisters, she flung her lifeline to the bed.

"You know, sometimes she gets on my nerves."

John had to laugh. And in a moment, so did big sister. "I can't believe I said that."

John made a long one and went to retrieve the balls. "Any more news from home?"

"Brock filed for divorce. Leslie is devastated."

He holed one from mid-range. "Who gets the Prius?"

"That's crass, John." But she laughed anew. What was getting into her? "Leslie, I'm sure."

After listening to the wife go on about a particular kitchen being too "eighties," the master (do hipsters have to abbreviate *everything*?) too closed off (whatever that meant), and the neighborhood too busy, John changed the channel.

Anchorwoman delivered the news. "It's being hailed by Pentagon sources as a dramatic new development in the War on Terror. The midnight raid by Army Rangers that apparently took the lives of Al Qaeda leader Sheikh Khalid Asad Wahid and several of his top lieutenants."

John paused his putting and turned to his live audience. "Another glorious victory in the perpetual war for peace."

"The Army has been unable to positively confirm the death of Sheikh Wahid, but according to an unnamed captain who took part in the raid, 'We got him.'"

"We're supposed to wave the flag now, and go yay," the golfer griped. "How many times have we heard this before? Huh? It's ten *thousand* miles from home. Who *cares*."

Gert nodded in agreement.

"Why are we still over there? I ask you. Except maybe to take the countries we've already destroyed, and reduce them to powder. It's no wonder they hate us." He gathered the remaining stray balls with his putter. "War without end. Amen."

Emily Upton was reported to be resting comfortably after her collapse at a rally in New York's Central Park. The secretary of state had reiterated her pledge to get tough with Russia, and that an Upton administration could send a clear message to Vladimir Putin—and further ensure stability in the Middle East—by bombing Iran. She had been hastily loaded into a waiting van after her little tumble, and hauled away; the clip playing over and over on conservative media. Nothing more than a touch of the flu, the press release read. Only a member of the vast right-wing conspiracy would suggest otherwise, respected pundits said.

Benjamin Jamaal Singh and Jim O'Leary had both pledged to select female running mates. One more win for America.

And the Republican front runner went on record in support of the controversial waterboarding technique. "I don't think we can exclude any form of enhanced interrogation when it comes to the defense of the lives and liberties of Americans from the threat of our sworn enemies."

"How about giving some of these so-called threats we've held for twenty years a fair trial, O'Leary?" John enjoined a shameless demagogue. "Isn't *that* the American way?"

A young journalist, obviously a noninitiate, put his microphone to O'Leary. "Senator, what is your response to those who maintain that the NSA's warrantless surveillance program is a threat to the very liberties you say you're trying to defend?"

Where did they find *this* kid? He would learn—or the gatekeepers would—soon enough.

The left side of O'Leary's face began to twitch. "In a post-9/11 world, and with the imminent danger of domestic terror, I think most Americans are in agreement that some loss of privacy may be necessary in order to combat these unseen threats."

John had about had his fill of this lizard. "You mean like all those phantom plots cooked up by the FBI?. . . *Huh!*. . .You neocon goons lie through your teeth. And you spy on law abiding Americans for god knows *what* reason. Who's the real threat, O'Leary?"

He pulled a wedge from his bag and turned to Gert. "I think Senator Police State would fit right in here."

"I can't believe I'm saying this," she admitted, "but you might be right."

She had an ironic little laugh.

# # #

The next day was one of rest and recovery. Two sixty-somethings had awakened to searing pain in muscles, and inoperable stiffness in joints they had long since forgotten.

"John, I can't walk!"

And her back was acting up again. After one of his special massages, supportive husband had helped her to the bathroom, where her morning passed in analgesic hot bath after taking the last of her Tylenol.

John found Mrs. Gilroy in the doldrums after the previous day's unrest, but she seemed to rally when he warmly assured her that order would soon be restored to her little burg.

"Thank you, Mr. Smith."

His walk downtown was more of a limp, but it was blessedly uneventful. Almost like being on vacation. He stopped periodically to stretch.

The front window of Jackie and Jill's had been boarded up, but a crudely painted sign announced to any it might concern that they were open for business. Someone had picked up all of the bagels. Probably Jackie and Jill.

He passed Mi Hong's—set to re-open the following week—the sad little man evidently having paid his debt to society. Thankfully, *they* would be long gone.

There was the church. He wondered what the services were like. Probably led by witches. He kept to the far side of the street.

The recycling center was overflowing with Asians wearing glasses, snapping photos of everything in sight. Interesting.

On an impulse he stopped at the pharmacy, and was able to procure their last bottle of Tylenol. He asked for a cup of water, and took two on the spot.

Admittedly no fan of the active lifestyle, peace was what John sought. He found it that day in the town square—stretched out on a grassy knoll with his books. He was soon asleep.

CHAPTER 13

Scary White Females

Sleep eluded him, but her rhythmic undertones told him he was alone. The blessing of that moment. Life could be a lot simpler without women around—aiding and abetting the confusion—but everywhere you looked, there they were. And they seemed to be in charge. They always have been, of course, whispering in their men's ears. That is where their real power lies. Smart women know this. The ultimate power has always been that exercised from *the shadows*. The rest is theater. When women attempt to beat men at their own game, they lose. Men are the stronger sex, and they quickly tire of shrill women. At some point, they will have had enough, and things would return to their natural order.

The disordered state of America—and the world—was no accident. And it was not a battle of ideologies. The left/right paradigm was, and always has been, a smokescreen. Surely, there were merits and drawbacks to the various systems of governance; but regardless of which of these was ostensibly in place in the various independent states, ostensibly chosen by the people of those states, the same cabal always came out on top.

The *plutocrats*. Wealth and power being one and the same. *Kleptocracy*, the underlying name of the game. They would wring from their subjects (the serfs), their every last drop of blood, sweat, and tears. The new world aristocracy adopting methods of aristocracies past. Now, in a world growing smaller by the day, their reach eclipsed borders. The *planet* was their oyster.

They rule by proxy. No need getting one's hands dirty. World domination is a messy business, with all the war, and privation, and bioweaponry. Our overlords jet to exotic mountain hideaways where, cloistered in ski lodges, they convene cozy coffee klatches, socially distanced from the hoi polloi, swapping family photos and mapping out the coming year in world events. Circumventing all those pesky elected governments—forever intent on sticking their collective nose into things. Working in concert, humanitarian-minded NGOs lend valuable foreign policy expertise, and those munificent tax-exempt foundations put their powers of persuasion (measured in Swiss francs) to work in setting policy. The cream of academia already on board, a roster of political and media mercenaries runs interference. Elites for hire. To those doing their bidding the plutocracy pays top dollar; and it's an equal opportunity employer. Narcissists; the intellectually vacant, and ethically void, are in high demand. The marvels of modern electronics and artifice at their command, the technocracy had conceived a brave new reality; confounding the body politic. While America slept—and consumed—they had taken their rightful place *sub rosa*. Eliminating one popular president who stood in their way, and stealing the election from another. *Ye shall be as gods.*

Whereas Republicans fussed over the scourge of socialism (while doing little to slow its march), John knew the demonstrable threat came from *authoritarianism. They* would tell the submissive when to leave home. Or take off the masks. *They* would tell the easily led which medicines to take, when, and how much. *They* would impose onerous new restrictions on business. And *they* would claim our children as their own.

The surest way to undermine a healthy civilization is to make it less civilized. Create moral chaos. Exchange the God of Heaven for the god of the material, and the glorification of self. Renounce everything good and decent in taking debauchery mainstream. For a free people all the old rules were just too confining. Substitute the wisdom of man. If we keep moving forward, has history not shown that things just get better and better? John recognized this thinking for what it was: the sovereign *myth of progress*. Life is not a dress rehearsal, say the knowing. Live for the now. Commercialize the whole of our being, right down to the genome. For every human need, let there be an app. But an economic system based on debt and constant war is nothing more than a mammoth Ponzi scheme. We have to keep spending—and America has to keep *fighting*—or the whole house of cards collapses.

The transformation, or reset, as envisioned by the technocrats, would not come overnight. The short-term agenda of the controlling class, John knew, was twofold: subvert a robust society by marginalizing its men; and to *divide*, the single aim of identity politics. And what could be a more efficient starting point than dividing humanity right down the middle? Proceeding from there to alienate black from white, red from blue, and young from old; pitting neighbor against neighbor, the haves against the have nots. Fear and envy the two most potent weapons ever unleashed on lesser humanity. The powers behind endless war without, stir conflict within. Social crises gestate within a twenty-four-hour news cycle, invariably attributed to the toxic white male. In global chess, the aggrieved *feminales* (what *was* their beef anyway?) mere pieces on the board, commoditized and monetized by the powers; like every other canonized victim class. In her misguided attempts to *seize* power, woman plays the dupe, and forfeits the leverage she has wielded from The Garden. Adam *listened* to Eve. Samson was helpless before Delilah. And, lest we forget, history records the beheading of John the Baptist on a woman's whim.

They were all over TV now—and in government—in positions of power formerly held by men. In the sixties they had discarded their bras, but for sports fan John the first salvo in the war on men came in the seventies, with Title IX. By an act of Congress women were put on a par with men. It made no difference that the *revenue* sports—the ones paying the freight—were played by men. Football, basketball, and at John's school, lacrosse. It was only fair. Men's track, wrestling, and swimming programs were dropped so the girls could play. Fairness, of course, had nothing to do with it.

Gert stirred, and he held his breath, but she picked up the beat momentarily. He thought of Mrs. Gilroy. The old girl had to sleep sometime, in all probability she and Gert in like dream, destination that brave world beyond far horizon where men knew their place.

Seeds are sown at the dawn of life. With the marketplace of highborn names having grown exponentially in recent decades, mothers looking to make a statement secure their little males' passage to nonbinary neverland with hypoallergenic names fit for a eunuch. An Aspen, Declan, or Indigo likely posed little threat to the testosteronical legacies of a John Wayne or John Wick. Or to the health, well-being, or dominion of the neighborhood tough. For the eco-alarmist sky is falling sect, organic options range from the popular Willow, River, or, John's current favorite, Rain; to the nettlesome Briar, or even, yes, Eden. Little skulls are forewarned not to conform to someone *else's* gender standards. The forward-thinking see the possibilities. Give them choices. Play house, not superheroes. Or dress-up! Grow the hair; paint the nails. Let them feel pretty. And who could say no to drag queen story time? What fun! In former (read *healthier)* times, this would have amounted to child abuse. Now it was loving affirmation for dysphoric four-year-olds—who best know their own bodies.

But for decades *real* mothers of sons had seen through the smoke, and spoken out about a war on boys. Pointy-headed educators had decided that letting boys be boys was disruptive in a learning environment. Take away their outlets—physical education and recess—said great minds. Drug them up. Make them docile and soft. Teach them to be more sensitive; like girls.

And it wasn't fair either that men had all the swell jobs—like doctors and mathematicians and CEOs and tech wizards. This just wouldn't do. Rather than ideals of home and hearth, girls should pursue careers. This would go against the female makeup, so they were reoriented to be more aggressive—like *boys*. For purposes of the debate, it was rebranded as *assertiveness*. Boys shot up on that strongest anti-boy drug of all: video games.

Driven then, girls went home each night to study hardy and chase the carrot. Boys racked up hits and kills and wins until breakfast. When girls struggled with math or science, and complained that boys were really better at that stuff, it was explained away as cultural bias. From crib to college, word came from on high that only the patriarchy stood in their way. You can do *anything*, girls! As long as a particular anything didn't involve parallel parking.

Role reversal was forerunner to the folly. Put the girls in shop, the boys in Home-ec. Get the girls in sports too. Sports fuel a competitive nature. Get them competing against boys when they're young, and more advanced in development. Embarrass the boys. Nothing is more damaging to a boy than losing to a *girl*. Let them get used to it. Forget that come puberty the girl wouldn't stand a chance. The damage to the boy's fragile ego is done. And girls are given a false sense of power.

It was a crime against humanity, this exploitation of the young. Children of both sexes need direction—from sane adults. It does not come naturally. The mind of the young male does not of itself turn to scholarship. It bounces all over the place. Natural aggressiveness has to be channeled. Sports help, but there has to be more. This is where that special teacher in every young person's life comes in. The one who identifies that peculiar spark. These days, righting past wrongs—or so they've been led to believe—they're all focused on the girls. John wondered what he might have been with a little guidance.

But he understood the manipulation of the American mind. Frontal assaults encounter resistance. That was where Leslie's incrementalism came in. Think tanks and academics work hand-in-hand with corporate media (and our upstanding intelligence agencies) pioneering techniques on how best to *think for us*. John recognized the process at work in bringing men to heel.

It went beyond social media. One need look no further than the billboards dotting the highway, feeding our subconscious. The ones telling girls to be *confident*! To *unleash their imaginations*! That they are *unstoppable*! Those for higher education, online courses, financial services, or—heaven help us—the military. All girls, all women, all the time.

In television commercials the selling of the product in question is secondary to the subliminal. Women shop, party, drive fast cars, or take exciting vacations, either alone or in groups. There they are—just the girls—having a blast. It's not clear if they're simply friends, or if there is something more going on. These days, who knows? Larger message: Guys? Who needs 'em?

The vanishing male. Even in the examples with staid old hetero couples, *she* is clearly the focus, the live wire, the one setting the pace; dude just along for the ride. Literally. She does the driving now.

Young women—wedding ring optional—are shown with their happy, well-adjusted children; father nowhere in sight. They boast of being problem solvers, another formerly male domain. Judging from the commercials, the white male, who used to succeed in business without really trying, is dead. He's been usurped by the hard charging modern woman who's goin' for it. The entrepreneurial spirit was alive and well in one known as Alex, star of the recent ad campaign for Mid-Atlantic Tranquility Bank. (Alex was formerly a *guy's* name, but has become a favorite of the manly white female.) While the white male underachiever slouches on couches watching football, Alex goes to work: making contacts, doing market studies, neighborhood outreach, and securing financing from Mid-Atlantic Tranquility Bank. Gearing up to launch her sustainable, socially responsible green enterprise. Unlike the loser boyfriend she just gave the heave-ho, Alex is possessed of the intestinal wherewithal to see it through to the finish. To build, from the ground up, an organization committed to excellence, and fairness in the workplace. Its mission not only to be inclusive, relevant, and fully vaxxed; but to turn a tidy profit. MATB salutes you, Alex!

For whatever reason, the ads for financial services are reliably the most noxious. We don't need men to support us, right? In John's personal favorite, a mother goes to buy a treat for her child (a little girl, naturally), but realizes she has misplaced her card. In steps a young woman—in the "butch" haircut from days of yore—with *her* card to save the day, and supplant the male in his role of hero.

It was about as subtle as a steamroller, yet John was astounded at the number of somnolent Americans who swallowed the propaganda whole. When he shared his observations with his wife, he was resentful of strides being made. Again with the fable of the strong woman.

Drawing on her own capacities, and with her understandable distaste for "controlling" men, where *does* this leave our strong woman? Alone, probably. In another ad, one of those women, a late fifty-something, meets with her investment adviser, an innocuous older male, planning her retirement. Well, girl, you did it all on your own. We're most proud. Now what?

With constant reinforcement, girls thrived on career aspirations, while boys languished. At some point assertive girls surged past the boys in the academic arena. But the anti-male offensive rolls on. In our colleges and universities, straight white males who resist—i.e., refuse to kneel—are harassed relentlessly. That's if they're "lucky" enough to get in. For highly qualified white and Asian males, admission to select institutions is a 50/50 proposition at best, but girls (along with other exalted victim brackets in toto) get the green light. They receive the lion's share of scholarships; so also, academic honors. Undergraduate women have outnumbered men in colleges and universities going on four decades—and they receive three *postgraduate* degrees for every two earned by men. Newsbabes and their neutered counterparts celebrated the happy numbers the week women officially surpassed men in employment. Why exactly was this cause for celebration? John dared to ask. More women than men now became lawyers and researchers and professors; and recruitment programs for women were "leveling the playing field" in tech. With the advantages white males had always enjoyed, this was only *fair*. Or so went the usual and customary hissy fit—in the face of mounting evidence to the contrary. Human perception perpetually behind the curve, the well-intentioned continued to champion girls long after the pendulum had swung to the opposite extreme. Girls were traveling in the fast lane; boys wandering aimlessly from neighborhood to neighborhood on skateboards.

The first female jockeys had come and gone. The first female race car drivers. Novelties, all. The first women in space—how many better qualified males passed over in the selection process? In California, high school girls wrestle against boys. What father in his right mind, John wondered, wants to see his teenage daughter groped in public by pubescent boys? Now some girls think they can play football. Their parents should be flayed.

Every "breakthrough" is cause for celebration; servile males leading the parade, flying high their feminist colors. If these women made it strictly on merit, John would have no complaint. He thought of his own sport, golf, where a handful of women have teed it up with the men at PGA tour events. Always to great fanfare, on shorter courses where they have a chance to compete. The catch? There you have to *earn* your way to the weekend. One young aspirant had the stated goal of winning The Masters—arguably the biggest prize in golf. To even *qualify* for The Masters, you have to win a PGA tour event. She never made a cut. Neither has any of the others.

For John, it was all a big yawn.

At what point does Woman declare victory? She is free now to do whatever she chooses. Disposing of that little intruder to the womb is cool—the Supreme Court and pious politicians tell us so. The *father* left with no say in the matter. She dominates newsrooms and Hollywood films, radio and television. She is more than likely your family doctor. Hiring preferences are the norm. She gets the jobs at the post office and UPS; while good manufacturing jobs, formerly performed by men, are outsourced or eliminated through automation. In short, she is the favorite for any job for which she applies. Physical standards are revised *downward*—so she can play cop. Or fireman. Or soldier. Female-owned businesses qualify for all means of tax breaks and other incentives. (Try getting a low-interest SBA loan as a white male.) She is the credible pitch person in all the commercials—white males conspicuous by their absence. She can drive a nail, handle a saw, and wield a sledgehammer. She films documentaries, writes how-to books, and does podcasts. She is an influencer. Funny then, that so many still seem so miserable.

John missed his mother. To her dying day she detested the man-haters. She said she never met a man who didn't treat her like a lady. It was because she *was* a lady. Lettered, and fiercely intelligent, she was content to be her husband's everything. To bring six children into the world—and raise them to responsible adulthood. In this she had left her mark.

"Men can't give birth," she told her daughters, "so they build bridges." The self-involved career woman has no time for children. She's tied up with bridge construction.

The only answer for these whiny women is more. To *have it all* is the grail, but, in the process, women are finding out what the men already knew. With the burdens of success—and the responsibility of providing for a family—come stress. One possible reason men commit suicide at a rate 4 1/2 times that of women. Getting to the top requires sacrifice. In leisure time. Family life. In *grandchildren*. Of one's very soul. Why aren't there more female CEOs they ask? Because—aside from the fact that men are better constituted to lead—historically, more women than men have decided it isn't worth it. Society thanks them. And to John it made no difference, the twaddle from the opinion-meisters. Women still want to raise families; and feel protected. And a society marked by weak men is poised for a fall.

Where *were* the men in that goofy place? John thought of how God had created them, male and female. The balance it provided—each there to temper the other's more destructive impulses. A world that denies its Creator gives us *gender*; effacing male and female, and the truth that He gave them distinct perspectives and purposes. *Vive la différence!*

John remembered the wisdom of Proverbs 31, from the days his mother had taken him to church. The mother of a King Lemuel asking "Who can find a virtuous woman, for her price is far above rubies?" Or in counterpoint, a heads-up for the unsuspecting male from King Solomon: "It is better to dwell in a corner of a roof, than in a house shared with a contentious woman." There were a lot of them around. But then the Bible was hopelessly outdated—to say nothing of sexist—and no longer relevant for the rule makers moving forward.

Today's emancipated woman looks hell-bent on proving she can make it without a man. Ironic, John thought. In his sixty-six years he had yet to come across a man who felt the same way. We *need* our mothers and our sisters, our wives and our daughters. To inspire us, to respect us, to *admire* us. To tell us we're stronger, or more handsome, or, in John's case, smarter than the other guy. To introduce *beauty* and *soft landings*, to our utilitarian, humdrum, male existence. We need her to take in our arms, to love and shelter; to spoil. To comfort her, and dry her tears. And she needs *us*—to whisper in her ear that everything's going to be all right. She makes us feel like it's all worth it. John thought back to high school, and his obsession with a certain Penelope. She of the dark eyes, shapely legs, and cryptic smile. Everything he did in those years (however modest his efforts) had, in whole or in part, been in the interest of his (ultimately doomed) quest for Penny's heart. All the witty little rhymes and parodies he had sent her way. Whatever the reference, no matter how obscure, she always got it. He lived for the sound of her laugh. Then she goes and marries some guy from Johns Hopkins who wasn't funny at all. Women. But then, trying to solve the eternal riddle was half the fun.

The woman behind the man is not a myth. How many Everests have been conquered by mighty men brought meekly to their knees by doe-eyed enchantresses? Without the women in our lives, men are left to run wild—*and we know it.* "Every wise woman buildeth her house; but the foolish plucketh it down with her hands." Women are the glue that hold it all together. Families; and a *people*.

But the pink brigades had taken the lead. Over digital highways and byways the social engineers plied their craft on the common conscious. They gave us the affable clowns in the commercials John loathed, rescued by their infallible women. The tough girls from movies and TV, little 110 pound actresses mixing it up with Trump supporters—and throwing them off rooftops. The action heroines (oops, that's *heroes* now) more powerful than speeding locomotives, able to leap tall buildings in a single bound. The one with guts is *always* the girl. Please.

But mind-numbed Americans take their nonsense at face value. The young especially, brimming with self-esteem, who, by right, simply know better. Critical thinkers suckled on corporate media pap. Or a Twittersphere ruled by skin-deep Hollywood know-nothings, and dumb athletes. Pretty faces and muscles minus any breath of meaningful education, or real-world IQ. People smart because they just . . . *are*.

World views are built upon sand. Shaped by late-night comics who long ago ceased being funny—or that morning talk show with the rotating bubbleheads. Tech chieftains screen access to material which might, for a thinking minority, unmask the inhuman face of oligarchy. The First Amendment? Who takes that literally?

Voters are herded to the polls—No ID? No problem!—who can't find Russia, China, or even the good ole U-S-of-A on a map. John's Scandinavian friend from college had laughed at "stupid Americans." It was embarrassing, because he was right. *Fifty years ago.* There should be a globe at the entrance to every polling place, John thought, and if you can't locate your *own country*, come back in a couple of years when you know something.

Men had only themselves to blame. *For putting up with it.* Doing the "gentlemanly" thing in rolling over, and letting the women walk all over them. Joining hands with the limp wrists—the first to surrender. The weasels cowering in the face of International Women's Day. Who shaved off their beards because a razor company told them they send the wrong message. The college pantywaists with their man buns, soft voices, swishy walks, and cute little backpacks. Tetrahydrocannabinol having replaced testosterone as active ingredient of choice for today's precious male.

He throws like a girl. *Lives* at Starbucks. He's quick to open up, and share his feelings, his vulnerabilities. (Women profess to love this, but laugh at the wuss behind his back.) Wary of being canceled, he tiptoes around these same women. Execrates the male establishment. In an Orwellian wrinkle, the weepy man is the strong man. John loved that one.

The rare animal with the stones to stand up to the female juggernaut is held up to riotous ridicule. Demands are issued for a public apology. He'll never work again in *this* town! they cry with glee.

Then came #metoo. The values police had struck again. Imagine, Hollywood and Washington swamp grotesqueries lecturing *us*. Harmless flirtation was out, and with it the last vestige of levity in the workplace. Chivalry not only dead, but had risen to the level of a high crime. "Girls were girls and men were men-n-n," Archie Bunker had crooned. No longer. The latter now hiding under their desks, guilty until proven innocent. John stopped watching the awards shows.

Ruminations in a dark room. A tiny flicker of light crept around the window shade, reflected on the screen of the little TV. He was reconciled to black-and-white now—transported to a time when everyone seemed happier. When right was right, and wrong was wrong. When *life* was more black-and-white. To be sure, a time before equal rights for many. He and Gert had marched for them. But a time when Black *families* were strong, their divorce rate the lowest of any ethnic group, and their neighborhoods the safest and cleanest in the major cities. Before the welfare state had so ably replaced fathers.

He remembered, as a boy, walking up the ramp at Memorial Stadium, half-expecting the field to be in black-and-white, and was stunned by how *green* it was. The bills of the Orioles' caps orange, just like on the baseball cards. He had laughed at his reaction, but it happened all over again the next time. Men went around in suits back then, and wore fedoras. Women wore dresses. People were polite. Everyone went to church. Maybe there was a connection.

That TV couple had been so dull, they were better suited to black-and-white anyway. Why was he letting them get to him? What was wrong with the world that it was the imbeciles who lived in the big houses?

He could make out the outline of his clubs, propped in the corner. Tomorrow.

# # #

Mrs. Gilroy was trying to communicate with José. She had just finished registering an unwary couple from Minnesota who seemed happy to be there.

"*Si*, José. The walk-in box?" She groped for *las palabras*. "Uh . . . compressor . . . no . . . *trabajo?*"

John, clubs slung over his shoulder, held the door for the Minnesotans as they passed through with smiles and luggage. Poor saps.

Mrs. Gilroy had José's full attention. "*Que es* walk-in box?"

"Walk-in box . . . *no esta frio*?" Oh, where were those *palabras*? "Compressor . . . uh . . . dripping . . . *agua*?"

"*Que es* dripping, Mrs. Gilroy?"

"Oh . . . *como se dice . . .*?

Lines of communication jammed for the present, John took the liberty. "Lovely morning, isn't it, Mrs. Gilroy?"

She had not noticed his entrance. Her face stiffened.

"*Perdóname*, José." She faced John. "Mr. Smith, if I could have a moment with you?"

He stopped. Downcast, Mrs. Gilroy dismissed José with a smile of apology, "*Hasta luego*, José."

José shrugged and left.

The mayor hung her head. She had failed. This was her town, the progressive New Jerusalem. Yes, she had given this brave immigrant sanctuary. But not *belonging*. She would accept full responsibility. Her failed interchange with the eager young Latino was a clarion call. "It's a travesty that we're not all taught Spanish from a young age."

His wife had called the mayor a visionary. John had been skeptical at the time, but now he saw the glimmer in those eyes. Her vision, the Progress of tomorrow, taking shape. Charged with emotion, she pounded the desk in declaring: "As of this moment, Progress is officially bilingual!" She fell into muse. "This could be a budget buster. I must speak with the borough council."

It was a transcendent moment—one of any number that week—but John had a tee-time. "You had something you wanted to talk about, Mrs. Gilroy?"

"Hmm? Oh. Yes." From the plastic strongbox, stowed in a secure location behind the desk, she retrieved a little paper ball, and held it up for John to see. "Mr. Smith, do you have any idea what this is?"

"It looks like a little ball of paper, Mrs. Gilroy."

It was unraveled to reveal Gert's empty salt packet. "This was discovered on the floor of the cafe at cleanup last night. In close proximity to the table where you and Mrs. Smith had been sitting."

John took the empty packet, and with furrowed brow examined it closely, front and back. "I see," he said, returning it to the mayor for safe-keeping. "Any leads?"

"Does it look in any way familiar?"

"Familiar?"

"Brittany said you two were behaving suspiciously."

John had never been so insulted. "Mrs. Gilroy. Are you implying . . . ?"

The mayor's tone was ominous. "You're aware of our laws, Mr. Smith. Let this serve as a word of warning." Whereupon she reverted to Chamber of Commerce happy face. "Enjoy your game!"

# # #

He had tried to explain golf to Gert. Golf was his escape. He didn't normally mean that in the literal sense, but on this occasion he had made his exit from the inn by way of the kitchen; the better to evade the Conscience.

Golf plugged holes in a man's life. If John were one to wax rhapsodic, he could sing the game's praises for the chance it gave urbanites to commune with nature. To get away from the wife and the guilt, to spend four quality hours with his pals. Or lyrical; the poetry recited to the hands by a shot hit dead flush. The miracle of flight, as the little white missile homed in on its target. To aspire; that sub-par round *was* out there, somewhere over the rainbow. To see what he was made of—two up with four to play, could he close it out? Even the hope of a second chance in life. What's a first-tee mulligan among friends? A time-honored tradition to be sure, but one that came with limits; for as every golfer knows, this greatest of all games doesn't build character, it *reveals* it.

The course was a pleasant surprise. Lush and nicely groomed. Remarkable that they could get something right, the superintendent evidently of the real world. There were no carts (strange), but then John didn't mind walking, his bag on a rented pull-cart. He had the place to himself. He could play two balls if he wanted. Two rounds for the price of one.

He stood on the first tee and took it all in. Breathed deep. This was living. He would take his time and relax. Just play one ball, and only hit a practice ball if needed. There was the expected touch of weirdness by way of the wooden sign planted beside the tee box: PLEASE BE CONSIDERATE OF THE RATTLESNAKES.

He swung a pair of irons to loosen up. Pulled his driver, practiced his setup, and took an inordinate number of practice swings, there being no one behind him to hold up.

He pulled a shiny new Titleist from his bag, and teed 'er high. After a few waggles, he gave it a mighty rip.

"Blocked it."

The shot was high—and fading. He watched it fly into some tall marsh grass.

"That one's gone."

Not a great start, but still he whistled happily as he strode the rough, coming to another sign, posted between the red stakes: NATURAL WETLAND—DO NOT ENTER!

He decided on the spot where his ball had entered the hazard, and dropped within the required two club-lengths. He pulled his 5-wood, taking only two practice swings this time. Made a decent swing and solid contact, but it was another high fade—"*Hang* on, baby!"—that he watched fly into the trees.

Oh, well. Maybe he could find it. He slid the club back in the bag and walked after his ball, undaunted. This was going to be a good day, no matter.

Bordering the woods, a third sign stood between John and his elusive ball: NATURE AREA—PROTECTED!—DO NOT ENTER.

It's inescapable. The tree-huggers haunt every corner of John's America, and seem to scare local politicians to death. The courses all have those dumb signs now, but no serious golfer pays any attention to them. If it ain't out of bounds, it's in play. He decided on an 8-iron for the punch-out, and checked to make sure the coast was clear before tiptoeing in. The little egg rested comfortably on the pine straw.

"There you are."

A tiny pine cone sat behind his ball. He leaned over to remove it, and—

"Freeze!"

The Chief stepped out from behind one of the massive trees. John remained bent over his ball. "Where the hell did you come from?"

"Hold that position." With steps officially procedural, The Chief took out her department iPhone, and with practiced precision began snapping from multiple angles. An open and shut case perhaps, but no stone would be left unturned in the investigation as she moved on to incriminating footprints. Photodocumentary phase complete, she put the phone back in its holster, and extended a beefy hand.

"ID."

"May I stand up now?"

"You may pick up your ball, and restore the pine cone to its original position, exactly as you found it."

When John played, he carried nothing in his pockets not golf-related. He fetched the wallet out of his bag, handed his license to The Chief, and she began the process.

"You have a cavalier attitude where it comes to delicate ecosystems, Mr. Smith," she said, awarding him his summons. From a second holster she removed another gadget and—*beep*—scanned the back of his license before handing it back. "And don't think we're not wise to you and your little salt caper."

She opened a plastic evidence bag with department logo.

"What?"

"I'll have to impound that ball."

"But it's a Pro V1."

"State's evidence, Mr. Smith. Used in the commission of an environmental offense."

He reluctantly dropped the ball in the bag.

"Have a good game," said The Chief, as she applied the tamper-proof seal.

# # #

The round went downhill from there. There was the towering 7-iron into the fourth green—"Get down!"—that carried all the way into the marsh grass behind it. What was up with the yardages? The drive he rinsed in the lake on five. The skulled pitch shot that rolled across the seventh green, down the shaved bank, and into the marsh grass. The damn stuff was everywhere.

By then he had torn up the scorecard. The final insult: In contravention of golf's most ancient custom, a guy couldn't even take a leak in peace. As he emerged from the trees on eight, zipping up, Officer McCoy was there, little hand out—

"ID."

But that was not the worst of it. The place was a swamp impersonating a golf course. After watching a beautifully struck 6-iron go to its demise in the marsh on thirteen, John picked up and walked home—convinced the environmentalists were *all* mental. That they hated golf, and golfers, and that this course was their revenge.

CHAPTER 14

Futbol Night!

Under an intense sun, Gert made her way back up Main Street in the direction of the inn, dress wet with perspiration. She fanned herself with the brochure: *Progress Recycling Center—Facts and Folklore.*

It had been a revelation, and an inspiration. Just when she was beginning to tire; of the fight; of the cause; that tour had replenished her spiritual stores. Its resources dwindling, her planet needed her. She would never again consign another recyclable to the trash. The message might even reach John, if she could just get him there.

But as she labored up the broken sidewalk—it really would be nice if they could do something about that—it was climate change foremost in her mind. Even the most intransigent of deniers—her ill-bred husband for one—couldn't argue in the face of such heat.

It took the last ounce of her strength to make it back to the inn. Mrs. Gilroy was on duty as per usual—crisp, dry, and cool as a cucumber. At times the woman really could be a bit much. The blades on her desk fan sat idle, the side window only cracked.

"Good afternoon, Mrs. Smith!"

What was the source of this woman's vitality? And what *do* they do with all that compost, anyway? Gert felt that she was about to faint.

"Yes, good afternoon, Mrs. Gilroy." She resumed her fanning. "It's so hot. I didn't know it got this hot."

"You're absolutely right, Mrs. Smith. It never gets this hot."

Not bothering to ask, Gert turned on the little fan, directing it in her face. "I think I'll go to our room and take a little nap to cool off."

"That sounds like an excellent idea, Mrs. Smith. You go right ahead and make yourself comfortable."

She started for their room.

"And Mrs. Smith…" Gert turned. "Tonight is *Futbol* Night!" Mrs. Gilroy exclaimed with a little shiver, switching off the fan.

Gert closed the windows immediately upon entering their room. Still fanning, she searched, scouring every nook and cranny for the thermostat she knew must be somewhere.

John entered, lugging his clubs.

"What are you doing back so soon?"

He plopped the bag in a corner. "I ran out of balls."

She checked the tiny closet, and behind the bed. Stood hipshot in the center of the room, only half-listening to her disconsolate other half, a man drained of body and spirit.

"A hundred and ninety-five bucks to play twelve holes." He pulled the two crumpled tickets from his pocket and tossed them onto the bureau. "Why'd you close the windows? It's hot as hell in here."

"I can't find the air conditioning."

As John embarked on an inspection tour of his own, Gert picked up the phone.

On the other end, Mrs. Gilroy answered. "Good afternoon, Progress Inn. Friday night is *Futbol* Night!" She listened. "Oh, good afternoon,

Mrs. Smith! . . . Mm-hmm . . . Yes, it is hot." She listened patiently as Gert explained their predicament.

"Air conditioning? Why, no, Mrs. Smith. Whoever said anything about air conditioning?"

# # #

Move that ball . . . move that ball . . . move that ball . . .

The room was bright, from a full moon, and the lights of the nearby *futbol* stadium. Curtains and windows had been thrown wide in hopes of capturing the chance breath of air. Under the slowly rotating ceiling fan, they lay sprawled on the bare sheet in their underwear.

Dee-fense (boom boom) . . . dee-fense (boom boom) . . . dee-fense (boom boom) . . .

Gert removed the folded washcloth from her forehead. "Can you get me some more ice?"

Move that ball . . . move that ball . . . move that ball . . .

"The machine's broken. I got that from the kitchen."

Dee-fense (boom boom) . . . dee-fense (boom boom) . . . dee-fense (boom boom) . . .

He had no idea of the stadium's size, but the deafening roars and deep-throated chants surely came from the Rose Bowl. Or the Colosseum—where Christians were served up for hungry lions. But then he wouldn't want to give these nutballs any ideas.

Move that ball . . . move that ball . . . move that ball . . .

On *Futbol* Night they cheered—or booed—*everything*. Could they not be a little more discriminating? But then that otherwise innocuous term came radioactive in the woke era.

Dee-fense (boom boom) . . . dee-fense (boom boom) . . . dee-fense (boom boom) . . .

"I wish there was a little more variety to those chants."

The amateurish band played nonstop discordant melodies from beneath their window.

"It's after midnight," Gert groaned.

"They've been playing for three"—John picked up the windup clock for a look—"and a half hours. Including the half-time show."

Move that ball . . . move that ball . . . move that ball . . ."

"What *was* that they were playing? I've never heard anything like it."

Dee-fense (boom boom) . . . dee-fense (boom boom) . . . dee-fense (boom boom) . . .

The incessant beat of the base drum followed the boys in lavender up and down the field; the *rat-a-tat* of the snare accompanying each deft move or pass; organ rhythms setting the pace. The beat picked up and a roar was taking hold—only to fade to a disappointed "Oooooooooooooh."

Gert still employed her brochure as a fan. "It's so hot."

Another roar. This one was serious. It built to a crescendo . . . and burst. A cannon fired, and the stadium announcer's voice boomed, "Gooooooooooooooallll!" There followed a sustained celebration of joy unbound—the insomniacs from a distant galaxy waiting for it all to end.

"Progress *Futbol* Club! The game is tied, one all. How about *that*, you gentlepeople of all genders."

John pictured doped-up snowflakes in an orgy of nonviolence. "Somebody score. Please. Do *not* go into overtime," he prayed.

Another cannon blast further fueled the frenzy. "We have Ooooooooooovertime!"

Fireworks filled the sky. The faithful gleefully sang along as the band—accompanied by the mad organist—struck up the glorious chorus of the excellent struggle. Impassioned lyrics gradually morphing into the chant feared round the league—

Pee Eff Cee . . . Pee Eff Cee . . . Pee Eff Cee . . .

Louder and louder it grew.

Pee Eff Cee . . . Pee Eff Cee . . . Pee Eff Cee . . .

"John?"

Pee Eff Cee . . . Pee Eff Cee . . . Pee Eff Cee . . .

"Hmm?"

Pee Eff Cee . . . Pee Eff Cee . . . Pee Eff Cee . . .

"I'm not enjoying this trip as much as I thought I would."

Pee Eff Cee . . . Pee Eff Cee . . . Pee Eff Cee . . .

"What?"

Pee Eff Cee . . . Pee Eff Cee . . . Pee Eff Cee . . .

"I said, I'm not enjoying this trip as much as I *thought* I would."

CHAPTER 15

Wedding Belles

They washed down their breakfasts, John with coffee, Gert with organic fruit juice. Survival instinct impelling them to consume *something*; with John crunching the numbers. The hours remaining before they could again eat real food. For some reason the McDonald's jingle was stuck in his head. Yes, they deserved a break.

The cafe was otherwise empty, except for the matronly diner two tables away, who was obviously Mrs. Gilroy in disguise.

"Why is that woman watching us?" Gert quietly asked her husband.

Mrs. Gilroy peered at them over the top of her menu. John spotted Officer McCoy peeking from behind the kitchen door. Gert leaned toward him and whispered—

"I think that's Mrs. Gilroy."

He whispered back. "Should I ask her to pass the salt?"

She slapped his hand.

"You would think The Chief would want to be in on a good stakeout."

"It's her wedding day, John." He had forgotten. He always forgot.

"That's right. Hagar gets hitched."

"She deserves to be happy, John. It's not ours to judge."

"Are you going?"

Mrs. Gilroy leaned in their direction, straining to pick up the conversation. Officer McCoy continued her surveillance.

"I don't know. If I did, what would you do?"

He thought about it.

# # #

"You can't just leave, John."

She loomed over him—the conscience he lacked—as he packed his bag. "Gert, this place differs from East Berlin in one important respect. All we have to do is walk out."

"But there's so much left to see."

"I'm gonna see if I can make the next plane outta here—if I have to *walk* to Eugene."

"What about all your fines?"

"I'll sneak out during the wedding."

"You'd leave me here all alone? What about my bags?" she pleaded, and for a moment she thought she had him.

"They have wheels, Gert."

"Please, John. It's only one more day."

He closed his bag and zipped it shut. "It's a vacation, my love, not a sentence."

With a slap of the tired old Oriole hat onto his tired old head, he took the little phone book from the night table and thumbed through it. "And from now on, I'm planning the trips." He dialed a number from the book, while his wife clutched pearls. "Yes, I'd like to order a cab."

Gert had a seat on the bed and started to cry. "What am I going to tell Leslie?"

"The Progress drop-off point." He listened. "Three hours?" He wrote the time on the pad. "Alright, if that's the best you can do. Thanks."

He hung up. She dabbed her eyes with a tissue. "You never even got to tour the recycling center."

"Youth is a blunder; manhood a struggle; old age a regret."

"Please, John," she sniffed. "As if H.L. Mencken knew a *thing* about a woman's feelings."

"Actually, it was Benjamin Disraeli."

"You're going to torture me with details at a time like this?"

He threw the phone book on the table. "Sort of sums up the whole week."

"Could we at least go for a walk?"

# # #

The sun was shining as they strolled down Main Street. John could have sworn several of the shops had closed just since his trip to the library. Gert found a souvenir shop that was still open and wanted to go inside, but he kept walking. This was one more vacation of which he wanted no reminders.

The bicycle traffic seemed light for a Saturday morning. Curiously, the resistance offered none. Anticlimactic for John. He had been girding for Armageddon.

They rounded the corner in time to witness the movement—in all its pride—spilling out of The Second Progress United Earth Church of Universal Love and Tolerance.

It was an extravaganza indeed. Red and yellow, black and white, the celebrants took flight. Festival spontaneous; statement extemporaneous.

A cavalcade of men in flowing gowns and tiaras; women in hard hats, denim, and work boots. Gender was someone else's hang-up. The province of the narrow. Those who stood in the way.

The barriers came down; borders open now. The borders of the heart. There *were* no boundaries, and they took full advantage. The emancipated came as cats and mice; kings and queens; angels and devils; wizards, and unicorns. A pageant of oaks and wildflowers and snowflakes. Larger-than-life penises and vaginae. In a performance to be remembered, Octavia led her Nude Shakespearean Players in their famous free dance.

Love was all that counted, and it was in bloom that day. Her Honor heralded the happy couple as they posed for a thousand phones—Sam luminous in white tie and tails, with top hat; The Chief's considerable assets on display in formal white gown and designer chains, blushing behind the veil, spikes of purple made over in a bedazzling pink for her big day.

They watched from a safe distance, Gert with little to say. "Oh, my."

Woman and wife—or whomever and whomever—descended the steps, showered in rice, pink popcorn, and lavender streamers. Air brimming with the essence of honeysuckle, roses, and lawns freshly mown; amidst peals of laughter and chords of "Pomp and Circumstance." To John's keen ear the violins only slightly off-key, played admirably by members of the Progress Band—high on grass and inclusion—which on this and like occasions doubled as the Progress Civic Orchestra. The Chief held Sam's hand as she climbed into the hansom.

"To each her own," John chortled.

Cheers and tears saw them off as they clip-clopped away, he cared not where.

In spectacle to evoke a Tim Burton nightmare, a crack of the snare launched the orchestra into "Let the Sunshine In"—accompanying Mrs. Gilroy's inspired soprano in a rousing rendition of the sixties anthem.

"Shall we dance?" John asked. Gert could only watch.

Euphoria taking hold, costumery was cast to the winds; and the merrymakers came together as one, in lusty expectation of the marital bed in the Age of Aquarius. The free clinic in nearby Coos Bay standing ready should any—in ecstasy's aftermath—require their services.

CHAPTER 16

An Enigma

In stealth fashion they passed through the office, toting bags and clubs, sparring in contentious murmurings.

"Leaving us?"

With this jolt to the connubial system, the focus shifted from incidental irritations, to the man behind the desk. *The Angel of Death*. With that lurid smile he could be no other. Gert dropped the two small bags she was carrying, brushing aside a single curl.

"Hello, Mister Gilroy."

"Good morning!"

John placed the room key on the desk. "Actually, we were going to check out, yes. Mr. and Mrs. Smith."

"Where's Mrs. Gilroy?" Gert was able to croak, parched vocal chords pressed into service.

Had he murdered her and stuffed her in some trunk? She was frozen, heart racing, measuring Mister Gilroy in the flesh, against the portrait a few feet away. His hair was clipped, gray now, the beard of shredded wheat. Dressed in green coveralls, he looked like a man who had shown up ready for a day's work. *Grave digging clothes.* Logging on to the computer, he seemed in full command of his faculties—but wasn't that always the way with the psychopath!

"I'm taking over here while she hosts that freak show wedding." His crooked smile was one tooth shy. "Of course, *she* doesn't know that." There was a trace of madness in his laugh.

They had seen, and in all manner heard, a healthy Mrs. Gilroy only an hour before. This gave Gert solace. Still, with the possible exception of her baby sister, in all her life she had never come face-to-face with an honest-to-God lunatic. She asked gently, "So, you're on leave from the hospital?"

She prayed he didn't have a gun. Of course, that would be preferable to a knife. Or an *axe.* There were more axes in Oregon than any other state! There had to be. If they were going to go, *please* let it be quick. Her life passed before her eyes. She hoped she had made a difference, but there was so much work left to be done. John had that usual dopey look on his face when he didn't know what to do.

"Let's just say that every once and a while I take my own leave."

He whistled happily while he worked. "Magic To Do" from *Pippin.* Imagine that. One of her favorites.

"Smith. I'm reviewing your account," he said, finding a particular screen. "Hmm. You two have been busy. Creating a public nuisance. Inciting a riot." He whistled through the gap. "It looks like we have, $1,750 in assorted fines; and, $900 for two missing bicycles and a pair of . . . *helmets?*"

"I forgot about the damn helmets," John snorted. "We can explain the bicycles."

Mister Gilroy scrolled, clicked, and looked up with a tickled grin. "No explanation necessary." This with a wink for Gert. "Anything else I can help you with?"

"What about John's fines?" Bolder now, with cash on the line.

"Let's see." Another look at the monitor. Two clicks later—"What fines?"

Gert looked pleased, and this pleased Mister Gilroy. He was enjoying this. He scrolled down. "Your original registration was for seven days, six nights. . ." On finding they'd been there for the better part of a week, he couldn't contain himself. "You two lasted six days in *this* nuthouse?"

John shrugged; humiliation total.

"I think you've got the record," he marveled, before adding insult to injury. "Wow. They should make a *commercial* with you two, or something." He drummed on the counter with a plastic ruler he was holding for some reason. "Let's check something here," he said, ruler in his teeth, eyes darting about the screen. "Well," he said, setting the ruler aside, "the very least we could do would be to credit your account for the final night." He looked up, happy to be of service to this sad sack pair. "It should appear on your next statement."

At that moment José entered, reacting to the sight of his former boss. "*Señor* Gilroy."

"*Hola, José. Por favor cuelgue apropiadamente ese signo que esta afuera en frente. Esta del reves. Y el compresor en el refrigerador con acceso directo todavia no trabaja. Puedes tomarle otra mirada, por favor?*"

"*Si, Señor Gilroy.*"

"*Gracias.*"

José left quickly. There was work to be done. Mister Gilroy flashed his Manson smile. "You two have a nice trip home. We hope to see you again soon."

# # #

Moribund Main Street stretched before them. They set their bags on the curb, Gert actually helping. Took in the sorry scape one last time.

"Will they be seeing us again anytime soon?" she asked.

"Interesting man, Mister Gilroy."

She rolled her formerly dysfunctional suitcase back and forth. "Nice of him to fix the wheel."

The long trek to freedom lay ahead. "Ready?"

She waltzed her way home, directing herself in song. Spotted John and Gert with their luggage. "Mrs. Smith!"

Her alarm was superseded by another—*this* coming from the direction of the bank. John laughed at the sight of the truck heading in their direction, cloud of dust in its wake.

"I like this guy's style."

Absconding Smiths in her sights, she let out her stride, pink gown streaming behind her. Forget the likely culprit in the latest robbery of the town bank—she was coming for them.

"Whatta we do now, Gert?"

She stuck out her thumb.

"What the hell are you doing?"

"He seemed nice enough."

The alleged perpetrator reflexively skidded to a stop; with doubts of his own. "Get in!" he snapped. Gert hopped in. John shrugged—what the hell—and threw their bags in the back. He jumped in and they went spinning out—the vanquished Mrs. Gilroy left dusty and forlorn.

Mister Gilroy had also decided to take his leave. He waved goodbye from the front steps of The Progress Inn—naked—but for his beaver hat, and an I(Heart)LA travel bag over his shoulder.

Through the rear window of the pickup, John spotted Officer McCoy and bike in vigorous pursuit. "Don't look now, but the law's after you."

The alleged perpetrator took a look in the mirror. "Shee-it. She don't scare me none." He turned to Gert. "I hope you don't think you're going to rehabilitate me, lady."

Under Gert's steady gaze he slowly revealed another side: an introspective mien, as it were. One of sadness even—what was going on *here*?—but with the faintest glint, of hope, in eyes of brown. "Y'all couldn't know this, but I come from a disadvantaged background."

John could see how this was going to play out.

His wife clutched the stranger's arm with unction, her heart broken to pieces by the bitter reality undergirding those words. America was a sewer, like Leslie always said, and this poor man was a casualty. *He* was not the criminal. She regarded the real criminal to her right—the one behind the stupid grin—with antipathy unmitigated. Fat, dumb, and happy in his white man's world.

She hadn't caught the glance, or the underlying devilry, that presumptive tragic figure had shot over her shoulder at his named oppressor. The barely discernible wink for John's benefit. What she could not miss, was the bag of money on the floor.

"But robbing banks. Why, young man?"

The alleged perpetrator laughed. "Cause that's where the money is."

John knew there was something he liked about this guy. As to whether catching a ride in a bank robber's getaway vehicle had been the prudent course, they would find out soon enough.

"But surely there's a better way," pleaded the one called to this place, at this point in time, to reclaim a wayward soul.

Presumably, the object of this magnanimity had come up against her kind before. "Lady, I don't need none of your savin'. This is *my* affirmative action plan." He couldn't help laughing at that turn of phrase. "One man against the power structure."

"Yes!" Gert burst forth. "You can join us in the fight." She positively glowed.

The alleged perpetrator shook his head with a crooked smile. "You woke types—like that fool mayor—weird me out, lady. Malcolm, before the government killed him, warned our people that if we know what's best, to stay away from you white liberals."

Despite his best efforts—he had to live with this woman—John laughed out loud.

"I'm just messin' with you lady. You can keep tryin'. I'm just letting you know I'm a free agent, and you ain't gettin' *me* on no plantation. Dr. Sowell says you people aspire to be our shepherds. But that requires us to be *sheep*."

As they bounced along the dirt road, it brought to John's mind another gem from the legendary economist, one all the Progress, Oregons of the world should commit to memory: "The road to despotism is paved with 'fairness.'"

They left Officer McCoy, and the borough of Progress, behind. John could feel the tension in his gut slowly recede. "Magic To Do" had replaced the McDonald's jingle in his inner jukebox. In college she had played that soundtrack until the grooves wore out.

About one thing the alleged perpetrator was contrite. "I do feel bad about robbing y'all."

Gert turned to John. "I knew he was nice."

"I ain't that nice."

John was plainly amused.

But to his wife this was no laughing matter. Her sensibilities called into question, this holy warrior had not yet begun to fight; the depth of her connection with their mystery outlier lost on that reptile.

Her eyes were on the gun now, resting on the seat between them. "Don't worry," the alleged perpetrator confessed, "it ain't loaded. But don't tell them people."

"We'll take it with us to the grave," John assured him.

The alleged perpetrator laughed, drumming on the wheel as they hit a smoother patch of road. John had an eye on his wife. She wasn't finished, not by a long shot. Her proprietary brand of compassion was irrepressible. The progressive never sleeps.

Gert's gift—Leslie had spoken of it—was her power of vision. A window to the inner recesses. This desperate man could laugh all he wanted, she could see through the denial. The pain radiating from eyes, shuttered from the world, yes; but that she clearly saw. He *needed* her, whether, for all his pride, he was willing to admit it to himself or not. "We don't even know your name, young man."

"Oh-ho-ho, no . . . You can just call me The Perpetrator."

"Give it up, Gert."

John looked their driver over. He had abandoned any hope of ascertaining the whys of this place, but here was an enigma, a man totally comfortable in his own skin. A sense of irony to match his humor. A rogue character who channels Malcolm X? Quotes *Thomas Sowell*? Did he have a family? Do they know what he does? Was there a dark, criminal past, or was that bank—sitting duck in the happy land of the snowflakes—purely a plum too sweet to resist? An unvarnished chain of armed robberies; or one man's private revolution?

They reached the drop-off point, and the cab was waiting. "Whattaya know," said John. "He's here."

The cabbie was opening the trunk as the truck skidded to a stop. John got out, pulling Gert with him. "Thanks for the ride."

The Perpetrator leaned across the seat. "How much?"

"What?"

"How much did I take from you two?"

What was this about? Was he into numbers? Did he keep detailed records for the IRS, just in case?

"Five hundred," John answered.

The Perpetrator delved into the bag on the floor, counted out ten fifties, and handed them to John.

Gert slapped her cynical other half on the wrist. "I told you he was nice."

"Don't worry, lady. There's plenty more where that came from."

John looked at the money in amazement. "Thanks. I guess." He stuffed the cash in his pocket, and went for their bags. Officer McCoy was a dot in the mirror, but drawing closer. And behind her—the invasion force! An angry brigade on bikes, Sensitive White Male leading the wave.

"You two better be movin' along. I got escapin' to do."

John spoke as he hoisted luggage. "I think we should do likewise. Technically, that money is stolen property."

"It's our money, John."

"I'd just as soon not have to make that distinction to a judge."

The Perpetrator sped off. The cabbie came over to help with the bags, and he and John lugged them to the car.

"It's wonderful to see you again, Milton," said Gert.

"Likewise, Mrs. Smith." As they reached the car he asked, "Who was that?"

"The crime spree that's hit Progress?" John replied with a grunt, throwing the first bag in the trunk. "He's it."

The rest were squeezed in, and the cabbie forced it shut. He grabbed John's clubs. "These can ride up front with me." He carried them around and threw them in the passenger seat. Then he took a step back, sizing up his two fares.

"Yeah, you two wearin' that beat down look," he said with a chuckle. "About like the rest of 'em." Gert had an idea as to what he was referring.

For her punch-drunk husband, it was a moment of renewal. The sough and sigh of quickening breezes rustled steeples of green that reached to the heavens. A cathedral of life's varied forms. *This* was what the brochure had promised. Birds sang from the treetops, others drifted on the current. He couldn't recall seeing a single bird in Progress. As if they knew.

"The sweet smell of freedom."

"Yes, sir," the cabbie was saying as he opened the door for Gert. "And I'll tell you something I wanted to tell you nice folks the night I brought y'all out here." With a single shake of his head, he pronounced: "Them women *scary*."

Gert got in, and he closed the door. "They'll take your money, too."

He and John walked around and got in from the other side. "They tried," exhaled the tired refugee, back from a week in the abyss. "Believe me, they tried."

The cabbie fired up the engine. "Where to?"

"The nearest steak house," said John, in charge now. "And step on it."

Whistle blast falling on deaf ears, an exasperated Officer McCoy, and assault group, hit the beach; only to watch helplessly as the cab sped away. Not far down the road, the freedom cab (as it would come to be remembered) was passed by the white van from The Meadows at Coos Bay, headed in the other direction. The various parties involved left to sort matters out.

John transferred cash from pocket to wallet, and rested his weary head on the back of the seat. The radio was on. "You know, Jennifer, there comes a time when you can no longer blame your adult problems on others," said the self-assured female voice. "Eventually you have to grow up, and be accountable for your own actions."

"That is sound advice," Gert mused. "Millie would do well to listen to this show."

"I thought you hated *Talk to Linda*."

"Is that who this is?"

"Actually," said her husband, "that's exactly who this is."

"I do . . . Well, I've never actually listened to her. But Leslie said that she was—"

John didn't need to hear the rest. He opened his window, and felt the blast in his face. There was life in the old boy yet. A single question remained—

"Milton, how far to Pebble Beach?"

CHAPTER 17

Moving *Fo-ward*

They made it to Pebble Beach in an SUV. A free upgrade from the compact rented from the company with the commercials with the guy John liked. On a beautiful sun-splashed day, John's dream of a lifetime had been fulfilled. The golf gods even consented to a momentary lull in the wind, facilitating his birdie on the picturesque seventh hole. The lone bright spot on a scorecard dominated by doubles, triples, and lost balls. Regardless, he had made a birdie at Pebble. He smiled the whole way home.

Their six days in Progress had put Gert's progressivism to the test, and John had seen signs of an awakening. In three days of Monterrey golf she had been the dutiful, submissive wife; happily piloting the cart up, down, and around, while her husband hacked up the beautiful courses. She was even giving him yardages. (Okay, they were right there on the screen in the cart, but still.)

But can a leopard ever really change her spots? Back home within the unyielding confines of the Beltway, Leslie, in league with the like-minded, had helped her recover her reason. Graciously regathered to the fold, Gert, in search of her best self, had crossed back over; though the compost project never really got off the ground. Literally. The pile topped out at nine inches. (John had measured it.) In retrospect, Gert looked back on their stay in Progress as a delight, informing John they would be returning over his dead body as soon as the town worked through a few issues.

He retired that fall, after forty-three years at EPA without ever making department head. They sold the house in Silver Spring, and moved to Naples. Florida, that is; into a condo bordering a golf course where he could play every day, commuting in his own cart. From where it was just a short hop to the Orioles' spring training home in Sarasota.

He could walk to the beach and read to his heart's content, with time now to further his H.L. Mencken studies. He began work on his memoir, *The Confessions of a Libertarian Mole in the EPA*, but abandoned the project after losing interest somewhere along the way.

Gert spent her days on the phone, conspiring with Leslie in the planned overthrow of the republic. She joined a move to petition the Florida Division of Elections to conduct a final audit of the 2000 presidential vote. They collected the required number of signatures, and their petition was granted; the subsequent recount resulting in Al Gore being declared the winner by a razor-thin margin.

The victorious would-be president formed an exploratory committee to plan his next move. He pledged American support for a revitalized Paris Climate Accord—and an undoing of the Iraq War.

Ted finally took Millie back, but now *she* was back at River Oaks.

It had always been assumed that Mrs. Gilroy would be mayor for life, but in a stunning upset she was turned from office that November. Octavia, running on twin planks of sweeping gender reform, and infrastructure improvements, had won in a landslide. She vowed to make Progress great again by making it the LGBT capital of the Pacific Northwest. She identified now as a polyamorous male, although the sight of the fair mayor calling on the various precincts in the altogether still aroused the support of the male cisgender community. She assured her constituents that any confusion could be resolved by attending her workshop—at $125 a pop. She further announced that, with the fiscal challenges facing the borough, the long-awaited field trip to San Francisco would be a virtual visit.

Out of a job, and with the fortunes of her little hostelry on the wane, Mrs. Gilroy took a part-time position as a greeter at the new Walmart—while secretly working the back channels at the zoning commission to have the store closed.

The Progress *Futbol* Club won its third straight division championship. Not quite as impressive as it sounds, there being only one other team in the Southern Division. On a sad note, with the fans getting restless, the league's first transgender coach was compassionately prevailed upon to move on—after they were also eliminated in the first round of the play-offs for the third straight year. She had filed a gender discrimination lawsuit, now before the Ninth Circuit.

Benjamin Jamaal Singh had been elected the nation's second African American, and *first* Jewish Hindu president, after receiving the Democratic nomination in a bitterly contested convention in Los Angeles. The night of her ultimate defeat, Emily Rogers Upton, in a drunken rage, had reportedly slung a bottle of bourbon at her philandering husband—former Senate majority leader Phil Upton—and torn a rotator cuff.

Another marriage hit the rocks, and this one rocked the community. Seeing the love of her life tormented by identity issues took a toll on the young bride, and after six months Sam was able to have her marriage annulled on a technicality when it was revealed The Chief had neglected to check the gender box on their wedding license application. She had married Rasheed Williams on the rebound. They met on Pride Night in Portland, the night the Bulls came to town. He had spotted her in the crowd, and upon meeting the seven-foot Chicago Bull, six-foot Sam had decided that, proud though she most certainly was, maybe she wasn't gay after all. She finally had a man she could look up to. Devastated, The Chief had suffered an emotional lockdown, and been forced to retire with full pension and benefits. She had shaved her head, removed her piercings, and taken a vow of chastity. Her new home was a corner suite on the second floor of Harmony House—four doors down from Mister Gilroy—at The Meadows at Coos Bay. She was content there. They had a gym. Octavia generously donated her services in private sessions. Officer McCoy became Chief McCoy.

Wilma Takes Washington was published in the spring.

Progress Federal was held up three more times before being forced to close its doors. The residents of the town now did their banking at the Wells Fargo branch in the new Walmart. They had a guard. The Perpetrator remained at large.

John resumed his reading.

And Al Gore's fate rested in the hands of the Supreme Court.

About the Author

R. SCOTT CORNWELL was born in Baltimore. White. Male. No apologies offered. He attended a respected university, but didn't learn much. He headed west, where he ended up writing five screenplays too smart for Hollywood. *#ScaryWhiteFemales* is his first novel. He lives on the wrong coast with his adoring wife, subsisting in a literary wasteland under the oppressive regime of Czar Newsom, *enfant terrible.*